"My brother is dead. He brought shame on all of us."

"And you're being punished for it," Bolan told the woman. He knew the ground rules of a classic vendetta. No survivors could be tolerated.

"My mother, aunts and uncles, cousins. Everyone. Gianni will not rest while any of us are alive."

"Gianni Magolino?"

She was staring at him now, eyes narrowed. "You know of him?"

Bolan rolled the dice. "I'm here because of him...because he killed your brother."

"I asked you if you are *polizia*," she accused him.

"And I'm not," Bolan assured her.

"What, then?"

"Someone who solves problems when the law breaks down."

MACK BOLAN ®

The Executioner

THE EXECUTIONER

DON PENDLETON'S

POINT BLANK

A GOLD EAGLE BOOK FROM

WORLDWIDE®

TORONTO • NEW YORK • LONDON
AMSTERDAM • PARIS • SYDNEY • HAMBURG
STOCKHOLM • ATHENS • TOKYO • MILAN
MADRID • WARSAW • BUDAPEST • AUCKLAND

For Prosecuting Magistrate Antonio Scopelliti
Assassinated on August 9, 1991

First edition December 2014

ISBN-13: 978-0-373-64433-9

Special thanks and acknowledgment to
Mike Newton for his contribution to this work.

Point Blank

Copyright © 2014 by Worldwide Library

Printed in U.S.A.

Crime leaves a trail like a water beetle;
Like a snail it leaves its shine;
Like a horse-mango it leaves its reek.
                              —Malayan proverb

I'm following a trail to those responsible for countless crimes.
The reek will be the smell of cleansing fire.
                              —Mack Bolan

THE
MACK BOLAN
LEGEND

Nothing less than a war could have fashioned the destiny of the man called Mack Bolan. Bolan earned the Executioner title in the jungle hell of Vietnam.

But this soldier also wore another name—Sergeant Mercy. He was so tagged because of the compassion he showed to wounded comrades-in-arms and Vietnamese civilians.

Mack Bolan's second tour of duty ended prematurely when he was given emergency leave to return home and bury his family, victims of the Mob. Then he declared a one-man war against the Mafia.

He confronted the Families head-on from coast to coast, and soon a hope of victory began to appear. But Bolan had broken society's every rule. That same society started gunning for this elusive warrior—to no avail.

So Bolan was offered amnesty to work within the system against terrorism. This time, as an employee of Uncle Sam, Bolan became Colonel John Phoenix. With a command center at Stony Man Farm in Virginia, he and his new allies—Able Team and Phoenix Force—waged relentless war on a new adversary: the KGB.

But when his one true love, April Rose, died at the hands of the Soviet terror machine, Bolan severed all ties with Establishment authority.

Now, after a lengthy lone-wolf struggle and much soul-searching, the Executioner has agreed to enter an "arm's-length" alliance with his government once more, reserving the right to pursue personal missions in his Everlasting War.

Prologue

Saturday—Shelter Island, New York

Rinaldo Natale felt lucky, and why shouldn't he? After twenty-odd years of the high life, doing whatever he wanted and thumbing his nose at the law, he'd dodged a guaranteed life sentence by rolling over on his longtime friends and partners. Granted, turning into an informant had its drawbacks, first and foremost being the automatic death penalty it carried. The American agents swore they could protect him, but Natale had his doubts. He'd seen enough informants killed at home, together with their families and friends, to know that no one, anywhere, was absolutely safe.

The good news was that Natale loved no one, except for himself. His wife was dead, they'd had no children and his mistress was already warming someone else's bed. As for blood relatives, they had disowned Natale when he'd made the choice to save himself and let the syndicate he'd served his entire adult life go to hell. They'd be among the first to kill him, given half a chance.

So much for family values.

The *other* good news was the safe house his protectors from the U.S. Marshals Service had selected for him. Shelter Island—how he loved the very name! One-third of the island was a virgin wilderness, the Mashomack Preserve. The year-round population was around twenty-five hundred people, many of whom golfed at the island's two country clubs or cruised around on their sailboats.

If anyone ventured into Smith Cove, on the island's south shore, they might speculate on who'd rented the rambling shorefront home abutting Mashomack Preserve. If they asked around, all they'd learn was that the place had been transformed into a posh executive's retreat.

Nonsense, of course, but they'd accept the explanation.

This week, four U.S. Marshals from the Witness Security Program were staying with Natale. They weren't exactly butlers, but they kept Natale fed and reasonably satisfied—although they'd drawn the line at renting him a woman.

He was planning to discuss that request once again this evening, over his veal parmigiana, wild mushrooms stuffed with ricotta, and red onions roasted under salt. If they refused again, Natale thought he might suggest obtaining several prostitutes, so they could share.

Something to think about.

Natale stepped out of the master bedroom's spacious shower and immediately felt that something in the house was...different. He listened for the television in the living room and heard the same news channel the marshals always listened to, unless there was a game on ESPN.

The television...but no voices.

Hastily, Natale dressed, sorry he wasn't allowed to possess any weapons other than the kitchen cutlery. His guards were armed, of course—one pistol each, together with a shotgun and an Uzi submachine gun—but that only helped Natale if they were alive and well when trouble came to call.

Speaking of calling, he could shout to his protectors, find out why they'd gone so deathly still, but some sixth sense advised him not to make a sound.

Should he investigate or flee? Escape meant knocking out a bedroom window screen or creeping through the house until he reached an exit. Either way, if trackers had located him, he'd be at risk.

But staying where he was might mean certain death.

Just nerves, Natale told himself. Not buying it, he reached for the doorknob.

DEPUTY U.S. MARSHAL Leo Torbett didn't usually care for babysitting duty, but covering Rinaldo Natale on the run-up to his trial appearance had turned into a fairly cushy gig. Torbett enjoyed first-rate Italian food—retrieved by car from Nonna's Trattoria in downtown Shelter Island—and he couldn't gripe about the ocean view. He *didn't* like the forest looming on the east side of the house, but there was nothing he could do about it, other than remaining on alert.

Torbett and his three men slept in shifts. At least two men were awake at all times, with their weapons ready. He also had a lookout at the ferry dock, which was supposedly the only way to reach the island.

So, sure, it made him nervous when a delivery truck pulled up out front, late afternoon, when he wasn't expecting a delivery.

"Look sharp, everybody," Torbett ordered, releasing the thumb-break catch on his Glock 22's high ride holster.

Natale was in the shower, sprucing up for dinner, but they didn't need to warn him yet. The delivery could be legitimate. Somebody from headquarters might have simply failed to call ahead, as protocol required. Another possibility was that the driver had the wrong address. It happened.

Or…

"Ed, kill the TV. Gary, get the door," Torbett said as he watched the delivery truck through one of two broad windows.

Ed Mulrooney switched the television off, while Gary Schuman crossed the living room in long strides, one hand on his Glock. He stooped a bit to watch the driveway through the peephole. "Getting out now, with a package," he announced.

Torbett could see the driver coming up the front walk and double-checking the address against the parcel he was carrying. He also had one of those pads that registered electronic signatures.

Why would headquarters pay a courier instead of sending someone from the Manhattan office? Torbett was considering that question when the driver seemed to stumble on the walkway's paving stones. The man got his balance back and pitched the parcel underhand, directly toward the window where Torbett stood.

He tried to shout "Watch out!" but it was already too late. The parcel detonated with a thunderclap that blew the picture window inward, driving shards of broken glass into his face.

NATALE HEARD THE blast and doubled back into his bedroom, slamming the door behind him. *Damn! No lock!* He ran toward the en suite bathroom. Hiding there was futile, but a window was set into the wall above the bathtub that might be large enough for him to squeeze through if he sucked in his gut and was willing to give up some skin.

Hell, yes, when the alternative was death.

Behind him, gunfire crackled, and he heard a man cry out in mortal pain. One of his watchdogs, or a member of the hit team?

In any case, it was clear the feds couldn't protect him. He was bailing out or meant to give it his best shot, at least. If he could make it to the woods, Natale thought he just might have a chance.

He cranked the bathroom window open wide, then punched its screen out with a quick one-two that left his knuckles raw. The next part would be difficult—crawling up and through the narrow window.

The shooting stopped. Footsteps approached his bedroom door, and someone opened it.

Not a marshal.

Standing in the bathtub, bitterly embarrassed that it had to end this way, Natale watched two men approach with compact submachine guns in their hands. He didn't recognize them. Why in hell should he?

"This is how a traitor dies," the taller man told him.

"No shit?" Natale sneered at them and rushed the guns, howling, before they opened up and blew him back into the bathtub. Into darkness everlasting, stained with crimson.

1

Tuesday—Catanzaro, Italy

Catanzaro is known for its "three Vs"—Saint Vitaliano, its patron saint; velvet and *vento,* the wind constantly blowing inland from the Ionian Sea. The capital of Calabria, at the toe of the Italian boot, teems with tourists in the summer months.

Mack Bolan, aka the Executioner, had not come to shop for velvet or idle on the beach. He was hunting for members of Calabria's native crime family, the 'Ndrangheta.

A mainland version of Sicily's Mafia, the 'Ndrangheta was equally venal and vicious, competing for its share of Italy's underground economy with the Neapolitan Camorra and the Apulian Sacra Corona Unita—the "United Sacred Crown." Between them, Italy's thriving syndicates had corrupted government, laundered money and murdered innocents.

None of which was Bolan's problem at the moment.

He was in Calabria, driving a rented Alfa Romeo Giulietta loaded with illegal weapons, because the 'Ndrangheta had reached across the Atlantic to the United States. Bolan intended to discourage that by any means required and drive the lesson home emphatically enough that it required no repetition.

He was a realist, of course. Bolan harbored no illusions

that he could eradicate the 'Ndrangheta, any more than he could wipe out evil from the world at large. What he could do—and *would* do—was treat the 'Ndrangheta to a dose of cleansing fire and make its members think twice about trying to infest America.

He had flown into Rome's Leonardo da Vinci–Fiumicino Airport, then shuttled down to Lamezia Terme International, located west of Catanzaro. From there, it was an easy drive into the capital and his appointment with an old auto mechanic who earned more money retailing weapons to the highest bidder than he ever had from tuning engines or relining brakes.

Bolan traveled with a bankroll he'd appropriated from the scavengers who made a mockery of civilized society. He could have tapped the till at Stony Man before he left the States, but robbing thieves and murderers and using their blood money against others like them held a strong appeal for Bolan.

Two birds, one stone.

Furio kept an arsenal on hand in his auto body shop for customers who needed hardware in a hurry without getting tangled in legal red tape. Bolan went for native brands, starting with a Beretta ARX-160 assault rifle chambered in 5.56 mm NATO, equipped with a folding stock, a Qioptiq VIPIR-2 thermal sight and a single-shot GLX160 grenade launcher. He backed that up with a Spectre M4 submachine gun and a Beretta 93R selective-fire pistol—both no longer in production but still deadly. Toss in spare magazines and ammunition, a dozen OD/82-SE fragmentation grenades, a fast-draw shoulder rig for the 93R, suppressors for the pistol and the Spectre, plus an ebony-handled switchblade stiletto sharpened to a razor's edge, and he was good to go.

Dressed to kill.

His next stop, as the sun set, was on Villa Fratelli Pllutino, where he planned to give some 'Ndrangheta members a preview of hell on Earth.

"THERE IS NO point in pleading for your life," Aldo Adamo declared.

"Pleading? Piece of shit!" the woman spat at him. "I plead for nothing."

"So, defiant to the end. At least you're not a coward, like your brother. He died whimpering."

"You lie!"

"I planned to make a video of his last moments, for your education, but we had to reconsider. Customs and the like. You understand."

"I understand what will become of you, Aldo, when Gianni hears what you have done to me."

Adamo laughed at that. "You're such a fool. Who do you think gave me the order?"

Blinking back at him, she hesitated, then replied, "I don't believe you."

"Foolish, as I said. Your family is tainted by his treachery. How could Gianni ever trust you—any of you—after the way Rinaldo betrayed him?"

Tears, the first he'd seen from her, shone on the woman's cheeks. "I'm not responsible for his mistakes," she said, her voice subdued now.

"No?" Adamo shrugged. "Perhaps not. But you know the rules. You've grown up in the *'ndrina* tradition. No betrayal can be tolerated. No risk of a personal vendetta may be overlooked. In your position, you could do more damage to the family than your *pentito* brother."

"I would never—"

"No, you won't," Adamo said. "It's my job to make sure of that."

It pleased him to watch as the last vestige of hope drained from her eyes. Her face, although still attractive, had a hollow look about it. She realized her time was running out, and there was nothing she could do or say to help herself.

Too bad, Adamo thought. Perhaps he should have given

her some hope and let her try to please him, as she had been pleasing his godfather for the past five years. But no, as the family's second in command, he had to carry out the orders he received. It was permissible for him to gloat at the whore's fall from grace, but he would go no further.

Stirring up Gianni Magolino's wrath at such a time might have dire results, even for him.

Adamo thought she was finished speaking, all her words exhausted, when she asked him, in a small voice, "What about my parents? And my brother?"

"That is for Gianni to decide," he answered. "Personally, in a case of treason, I prefer to wipe out root and branch."

She sobbed. "Celino is only a child, ten years old."

"Old enough to remember. I killed my first man at age twelve," Adamo said and smiled at the sweet memory.

She glowered at him through a sheen of tears. "Spare them," she said, "and I will do whatever you desire. I've seen the way you watch me when Gianni's back is turned."

Adamo saw the trap and skirted it. "Such vanity," he said, sneering. "Of course, I cannot blame you, trying to employ your only talent, but it's wasted here."

"Is it?" She almost smiled now. "Was I wrong about you? Do you prefer men after all?"

She was laughing at him when Adamo slapped her, pitched her from the metal folding chair she occupied and sent her sprawling to the floor. She could not break her fall, hands tied behind her as they were, and when she stared up at him, he was pleased to see blood at the corner of her mouth.

Reaching down, Adamo clutched one of the woman's arms and hauled her to her feet, ignoring her sharp gasp of pain as he twisted her elbow and shoulder. Planted firmly on her feet once more, she tried to kick him, but he turned aside and slammed a fist into her face. She dropped again, weeping. This time, Adamo left her on the floor.

He pressed a button on the intercom atop his desk, and

three of his men entered, barely glancing at the fallen woman while they waited for instructions. "Take her to the pier," Adamo said. "I have the *Mare Strega* waiting for you. Go out a mile or two and feed her to the fishes, eh?"

"Yes, sir," one of them said, the others standing mute on either side of him.

Two of them picked the woman up as if she weighed nothing, supporting her between them as they left Adamo's office, with the third man bringing up the rear. Still seething from the insult she had hurled at him, Adamo took some consolation from the fact that he would never see her face or hear her mocking voice again.

"Sleep with the fishes," he advised her fading memory and gladly turned his mind to other things.

BOLAN WAS PROCEEDING CAUTIOUSLY. The modest block of offices he was looking for, on Via Nuova, listed Aldo Adamo among its tenants. Ranked as number two in the major companies of the 'Ndrangheta, Adamo would make a decent target for the start of Bolan's blitz. With one stroke, Bolan would send a message, letting every member of the rotten family know that nobody was safe.

Psywar. Or, as the Pentagon was pleased to call it lately, shock and awe. It all came down to killing with a purpose.

Some things never change.

He looped around curving one-way streets to catch Vialle dei Normanni, circling north again to pick up Via Nuova southbound. Streets in Catanzaro were a winding maze, where the traffic alternately surged and stalled. Some drivers kept the pedal down regardless, blaring their horns at anyone who tried to drive the speed limit, while others poked along, searching for addresses they never seemed to find. Trucks were the wild card, belching diesel smoke and straddling lanes or blocking traffic to unload their cargo as the spirit moved them.

Bolan took it all in stride. He had no deadline for his

drop-in on Adamo, and he wasn't even sure the mobster would be there when he arrived, but either way, the Executioner would leave a message for the 'Ndrangheta in a language its goons could understand.

Although the 'Ndrangheta owned the building he was headed for, other tenants could be in the line of fire—most of them innocent—if things got out of hand. Bolan didn't plan on leveling the place or hosing it with automatic fire, but he thought it would be nice to stop and introduce himself, after a fashion, to the men who thought they owned the city.

The Executioner's present life had started with a one-man war against the likes of Catanzaro's parasites—bloodsuckers who infected everyone and everything they touched. Negotiation was impossible with ticks, lice, gangsters—choose your vermin. Bolan couldn't purge the plague forever, as researchers claimed they'd done with smallpox, but he could provide a dose of topical relief and give the authorities—the decent, honest ones—a chance to do their jobs.

And if the scourge returned, if Bolan survived that long, he could return and do it all again.

Bolan rolled along the snaky path of Via Nuova, following a bus that smelled more like a garbage truck, until he spied the address he was looking for. A side street let him duck through a strip mall's parking lot and double back to find a parking space that let him watch the building. Bolan checked out security and studied nearby pedestrians for any sign that they were cops or mobsters.

Both posed problems for him, one being a target, whereas the other was an obstacle. At the beginning of his lonely war, Bolan had vowed he would never kill a cop, regardless of the circumstances. Plainclothes detectives were a headache because they might shoot first without announcing who they were, and Bolan didn't want to take a chance on dropping one of them by accident.

But the building's entrance was clear—as far as he could see—until three no-neck types emerged, marching a woman toward the street. She sagged between them, and they held her up by her arms, which seemed to be secured behind her back. As Bolan watched, a car pulled up to meet the four, and they deposited their captive in the backseat before climbing in to sandwich her and close the doors.

Game change.

As the sedan rolled out, Bolan gave it a block, then started following.

Why not? If he could sting the 'Ndrangheta with a rescue operation, it was worth a shot.

Besides, he'd always been a sucker for a damsel in distress.

"WHERE ARE WE taking her?" asked Dino Terranova, in the driver's seat.

"The boat," Fausto Cortale said. "She's going for a swim."

"Too bad," Ruggiero Aiello chimed in. "Seems like a waste."

Cortale grunted in response. He had a date lined up for later in the evening, and he did not want to dawdle with their prisoner. Load her aboard the *Mare Strega,* cruise a few miles out to sea and leave her with a bullet in her head, maybe a gym bag filled with scrap iron tied around her ankles. By the time she floated up again, if ever, there'd be next to nothing left for lab analysis.

And if she was identified someday, so what? A boss's mistress disappeared and later turned up dead. Who cared? By then, her family would be extinct and life would have returned to normal, as it was before her brother had betrayed the family.

Knowing who had wiped out the Natale clan was one thing; proving it was something else entirely. It was good for word to get around. Making examples was the best way to prevent prospective rats from talking out of turn.

Still, now that he was sitting close to her, their thighs pressing together....

"It's a waste, all right," Gitano Malara echoed, resting one of his hands on the prisoner's other leg. "We ought to stop somewhere and have a little party, eh?"

"You don't mind, do you, *bella?*" Terranova asked, angling for a quick look in the rearview mirror.

"She don't mind," Aiello said. "Lets her live a little longer anyway."

"That's right," Malara said. "I bet she'd be real grateful."

"Have you seen a mirror lately?" Cortale asked him.

"Hey!"

But it was getting to him, sitting close to her and hearing all the bawdy talk, knowing they could take her anywhere they wanted, make her do anything, as long as she still wound up feeding fish. Aldo would never know the difference if Cortale swore them all to silence under pain of death.

They wouldn't even have to deviate from Aldo's plan. The boat was waiting for them. Once they had put out to sea, there would be nothing, no one, to distract them.

Trying to keep it casual, he let his left hand come to rest on her right thigh. She tried to squirm away from him, but there was nowhere she could go, trapped with Malara to her left. She made a whiny noise but couldn't even push his hand away because hers were tied behind her back.

The possibilities aroused Cortale, inflaming him.

"Hey, Fausto." Terranova's voice cut through his steamy thoughts. "I think we got a tail."

"The hell you mean, a tail?"

"Just what I said. I've had an eye on this one Alfa, trailing us since we left Aldo's."

They were rolling southbound, toward the coast, along Viale degli Angioini, and although the flow of cars was still substantial, Cortale knew they'd lost a fair number of the vehicles that had surrounded them as they were leaving Catanzaro.

"We do something, you'd better be damn sure," he cautioned Terranova. "It comes down to you."

"I'm sure," Terranova replied.

"All right, then. Lead him off on Via Solferino when you get there, and we'll find a place to take him."

Cortale felt his rutting mood go sour, changing into something else—a killing frame of mind. And that wasn't so strange. Weren't sex and death closely related, after all?

BOLAN HAD NO idea where the mobsters were taking their prisoner, whether their destination lay somewhere in the open countryside south of Catanzaro, or if they were on their way to the coast. Either option offered places to dispose of a body—a shallow grave in some lonely field or a burial at sea. He was gambling that they wouldn't kill her in the car and risk soiling their clothes or the upholstery, but even that could not be guaranteed.

She could be dead already, maybe finished off with a garrote, as many Old World killers still preferred to do when it was feasible. No noise, no mess to speak of if you did it properly. There was a chance he couldn't save the lady—that he might only be able to avenge her—but he kept betting that she'd be easier to handle while alive, up to the moment when they'd reached her final destination.

Traffic was thinning as they pulled away from Catanzaro, with commuters peeling off toward their suburban homes, replaced by others on their way down to the seashore. Bolan hung back in the wake of the sedan, knowing they might have spotted him but hoping otherwise. If he was burned, they'd done nothing so far to indicate as much, but he could only wait and see.

When the 'Ndrangheta driver started signaling a left turn just beyond a road sign for the village of Le Croci,

Bolan kept his signal off and slowed down to let a van slide in between his Alfa and the car he was pursuing—just a little twist to calm suspicion if the hit team thought they had a tail. He'd follow them, but he didn't want to tip them off.

Bolan made his turn at the last minute, ignored a bleating horn behind him, and began to track his target on the winding two-lane road. No other vehicles were between them now. He let the mob car lead him by four hundred yards but still knew he was clearly visible behind them if they bothered looking back.

The trick was to keep from spooking them but still be quick enough to intervene when they reached their destination and prepared to dispose of their prisoner. Hanging back a quarter of a mile delayed Bolan's reaction time, but he'd alert his adversaries in a heartbeat if he roared up on their bumper when they'd stopped to drag the lady from their car. Moving too soon could get her killed. Likewise, moving too late could have the same result.

The land around them now was mostly open, with large homes on multiple acres on the southern side. Beyond the houses, he glimpsed orchards, whereas the fields across the road stood fallow and awaiting cultivation. Not the best place for a firefight, but he was grateful for the open space and scarcity of innocents. If his intended targets led him to a better killing ground, he'd thank them for it.

When the smoke cleared.

And the lady? Bolan hadn't thought that far ahead. He'd seen her and decided he would help her if he could. Beyond that, once he'd freed her from captivity, she could decide what happened next—up to a point. He wasn't anybody's nursemaid, and he had no time to care for the woman. If he could find someone reliable to take her off his hands, he'd go with that.

If not…well, he could put her on a plane to anywhere outside Calabria, give her a head start at the very least. It was a better chance than anything awaiting her right now.

Speeding up a little, Bolan reached inside his jacket, checking the Beretta in its quick-draw holster. It was ready, as was he.

The game was on in earnest now. And there was going to be blood.

2

Monday—National Museum of Crime & Punishment, Washington, D.C.

This has to be a joke, Bolan thought. But Hal Brognola, who worked at the U.S. Department of Justice, had proposed the meeting place, so Bolan handed some bills to a clerk behind the sales counter. He cleared the turnstile and passed through a mock medieval dungeon filled with torture devices into a room where a 1930s-era car sat behind velvet ropes, its windows and its paint job shot to hell.

Bolan ignored the serial killers gallery, slack-jawed faces watching him from eight-by-ten mug shots as he walked by. Hal had suggested meeting at the mob exhibit, and he saw it up ahead. More mug shots and blow-ups of newspaper clippings, an Uzi submachine gun next to a fedora and a photo of the neon sign from the original Flamingo hotel and casino, erected by Bugsy Siegel in Las Vegas. Bolan found the display more in tune with Hollywood's portrayal of the underworld than anything he'd faced in real life.

Hal Brognola suddenly appeared at his elbow. "Let's take a walk."

They left gangland behind and ambled toward the museum's CSI lab, where a mannequin lay on an operating table. Behind it stood displays on toxicology, dental I.D. procedures and the like.

"This must be like a busman's holiday for you," Brognola said.

"It cost me twenty-one ninety-five."

"I get a discount with my badge."

"Congratulations."

"So, what do you know about the 'Ndrangheta?" Hal asked, cutting to the chase.

"One of the top syndicates in Italy," Bolan replied. "Sometimes they collaborate with the Camorra and the Mafia. When that breaks down, they fight. They're less well known than the Mafia but just as dangerous."

"And not confined to Italy these days," Brognola said. "They're everywhere in Europe, east and west. They've also started cropping up in Canada, the States, down into Mexico, Colombia and Argentina. Hell, they're even in Australia. Worldwide, we estimate they're banking close to fifty *billion* annually. Much of that derives from trafficking in drugs. The rest, you name it: weapons, vice, loan-sharking and extortion, public contracts and so-called legitimate business."

Nothing Hal had said so far was a surprise. Bolan walked beside him, letting him get to the point in his own good time.

"Two days ago, there was a shootout on Shelter Island. Well, a massacre's more like it. Did you catch the news?"

"Some marshals and a witness," Bolan said.

"Affirmative. Four deputy U.S. Marshals blown away while watching over one Rinaldo Natale, scheduled to testify next week in New York at the racketeering trial of three high-ranking *'ndranghetisti*. Without him, let's just say the prosecution's sweating."

"The time to call would've been before Natale bit the dust," Bolan observed.

"Agreed. But spilled milk and all that. Anyway, we need to send a message back to the Old Country."

"You know who gave the order?"

"Ninety-nine percent sure I do."

"Okay," Bolan said. "Tell me."

"He's Gianni Magolino, the *capobastone* of one of the strongest, if not *the* strongest, *'ndrina* families in the area."

"I'm with you so far."

"His lieutenants are the men awaiting trial in Manhattan."

"So he has a solid foothold in the States?" Bolan asked.

"Aside from New York, he's got people in Florida, Nevada, Southern California—and El Paso."

"Ciudad Juárez," Bolan replied.

"No doubt."

The border city, with its countless unsolved murders, was a major gateway for narcotics passing out of Mexico and through El Paso, Texas.

"Any chance of working with the locals in Calabria?" Bolan asked, feeling fairly sure he already knew the answer to his question.

"You know how they are," Brognola replied. "All good intentions on the surface, and a few hard-chargers in the ranks, but they get weeded out. Their DIA—the anti-Mafia investigators—has had a couple of its top men operating underground for fifteen, twenty years, but no one's gotten close to Magolino so far."

"Okay," Bolan said. "So, I guess you need me out there yesterday."

"Tomorrow's soon enough." Brognola handed him a USB key he'd fished out of a pocket. "Here's a little homework for the flight."

THE TRAVEL PREPARATIONS didn't take much time. With an afternoon departure from Washington, Bolan made his way to the airport and spent his time there reviewing the information from Hal's flash drive.

It turned out that the 'Ndrangheta had been operating since the 1860s. Its structure was similar to that of

the Mafia, with strong emphasis on family and faith.
The sons of members were christened at birth as *giovane
d'onore*, "youth of honor," expected to follow in their fa-
thers' footsteps. At age fourteen they graduated to *pic-
ciotto d'onore*—"children of honor"—indoctrinated into
blind obedience and tasked with jobs considered "child's
play." The next rung up the ladder, *camorrista*, brought
more serious duties. *Sgarrista* was the highest rank of the
'Ndrangheta's *Società Minore* and was as far as some members ever advanced.

The next step—into the *Società Maggiore*—made the
member a *Santista*, or "saint," the first degree of full mem-
bership. Above the saints stood *vangelo*—"gospels"—*quar-
tino, trequartino* and *padrino. Padrino was the* Godfather.
Bolan realized much of the ceremony was simply for show.
The *'ndranghetisti* made a mockery of Italy's traditional
religion and the values normally ascribed to family. For
all their talk of sins against the family and stained honor,
members of the 'Ndrangheta lived by a savage code of silence enforced by murder. They were no different than any
other criminal or terrorist Bolan had confronted in the past,
and they deserved no mercy from the Executioner.

Bolan turned his attention to the Magolino family in
Catanzaro. Its *padrino* for the past ten years was one
Gianni Magolino, forty-six years old. He had logged his
first arrest in 1985, at age seventeen, for attempted murder—a charge dismissed after the victim and four witnesses refused to testify. From there, his rap sheet read
like a menu of crime: armed robbery, extortion, aggravated
assault, suspicion of drug trafficking, suspicion of gun-
running and suspicion of murder (three counts). The only
charge that stuck was one for operating an illegal casino.
In that case, Magolino had served sixty days and paid a
fine of ten thousand lira—about seven American dollars.

That kind of wrist-slap had taught Magolino that crime
did pay. He'd clawed his way up to command the former

Iamonte family, aided by longtime friend and current *tre-quartino,* Aldo Adamo. Four years Magolino's junior and as ruthless as they came, Adamo was suspected by authorities of more than forty homicides. Most of his victims had been rival *'ndranghetisti,* but the list also included two former girlfriends, a cousin and his stepfather. Adamo knew where the bodies were buried, and he'd planted some of them himself.

Together, Magolino and Adamo presided over an estimated four hundred soldiers, with outposts in Spain, Belgium, London, the United States and Mexico. Hal's digging had turned up a list of friendly coppers in Calabria's police along with suspected collaborators inside the *Guardia di Finanza,* a military corps attached to the Ministry of Economy and Finance charged with conducting anti-Mafia operations.

One rotten apple in that barrel could alert *'ndranghetisti* to impending prosecutions and allow them to tamper with state's evidence and mark potential witnesses for execution. Multiply that rotten apple by a dozen or a hundred, and it came as no surprise when top-flight mobsters walked away from court unscathed, time after time.

But living through a Bolan blitz was something else entirely.

As the Maglioni organization was about to learn.

Bolan would be traveling to Italy as Scott Parker, a businessman from Baltimore with diverse interests in petroleum, real estate and information technology. His passport was impeccable, as was the Maryland driver's license, Platinum American Express card and the matching Platinum Visa. Any background check on "Parker" would reveal two years of military service in his teens, a B.A. in business administration from UM-Baltimore and a solid stock portfolio. As CEO of Parker International, he had the time and wherewithal to travel as he pleased, for business and for pleasure.

This would not be Bolan's first trip to Italy, by any means. Even before his public "death" in New York City, while Brognola's Stony Man project was still on the drawing board, Bolan had paid a hellfire visit to Sicily, ancestral home of the Mafia, reminding its godfathers that they were not untouchable. Since then, he'd been back several times, pursuing different angles in the war on terrorism but returning now brought on a flashback to old times.

It never failed. A mention of the Mafia, or any of the syndicates that mimicked it under other names, brought back the nightmare that had devastated Bolan's family and launched him into a crusade he'd never imagined as a young man. Bolan had been a Green Beret, on track to a distinguished lifer's career in the military, when he'd lost three-quarters of his family, only his younger brother still alive to tell a tale of murder-suicide provoked by vicious loan sharks. Bolan—already tagged as "The Executioner" for his cold eye and steady hand in battle—had settled that score, then decided personal vengeance fell short of the mark. A whole class of parasites still fed on society's blood.

Old times, bad times—but what had changed?

Bolan was not religious, in the normal sense. He didn't shun the notion of a higher power or discount any particular creed at a glance, but if he'd learned one thing from a lifetime of struggle, it was that predators never relented. They might "find the Lord" to impress a parole board, but once they hit the streets again, 99.99 percent reverted to their old ways.

Long story short, the only cure for evil was extinction.

And the Magolino organization's day was coming.

Bolan's flight to Rome lifted off from Dulles more or less on time, and it would be eight hours and forty-one minutes from takeoff to touchdown, nonstop. The long flight gave him time to sleep. Downtime was a rare commodity in Bolan's world, and he took full advantage of it when he could.

As far as planning went, he'd done all he could before his feet were on Italian soil. He had a rental car lined up, along with weapons if the dealer didn't sell him out. Beyond that, he had targets and certain thoughts on how he should proceed, but plans were always transient in battle. They changed by the day, by the minute, forcing warriors to adapt or die.

And Bolan was a master when it came to adapting.

He'd hit the ground running, begin with a blitz and be ready for whatever happened from there. Take the war to his enemies, grinding them down with no quarter.

Bolan had had an hour to kill at the terminal in Rome, before his Alitalia flight took off for Lamezia Terme. Time enough for him to drift along the concourse, eavesdropping on conversations as he passed, translating them with the Italian he had learned while hunting monsters who defiled their race's ancient, honorable reputation with the taint of crime. When he stopped to order coffee, overpriced but hot and strong, he'd engaged in conversation with the girl behind the counter, raising no eyebrows.

No one in Catanzaro would mistake him for a native, but he could communicate without an interpreter, and that was all Bolan required. Beyond the basics, he would let his weapons do his talking, confident his enemies would get the message.

Hal's instructions were explicit: crush the Magolino family and leave it beaten to the point that, if it managed to survive, it would refrain from planting any more flags in the States. Drive home that message in the classic Bolan style, while still preserving plausible deniability.

If he was captured, naturally, Hal would have to cut him loose. If Bolan died in battle, there would be no record of him in the files at Stony Man, in Washington, or anywhere at all. His second passing might evoke some tears, but life went on. The *fight* went on. Survivors couldn't do their best if they were burdened by the memories of those who'd fallen along the way. It was a soldier's life, willingly accepted by those few who made the cut.

He had another chance to try out his Italian at the auto rental booth in Lamezia Terme. His second test subject, a young man with a mop of curly hair and the pathetic ghost of a mustache, appeared to have no trouble understanding anything Bolan said. More to the point, his answers to some routine questions, given back in rapid-fire, came through to Bolan loud and clear.

Ten minutes later, he was on the road, eastbound, toward his final destination. One more stop, to arm himself, and he'd be ready for anything.

But was the 'Ndrangheta ready for the Executioner?

3

Tuesday—Le Croci, Calabria

"Still with us," Terranova said.

Cortale swiveled in his seat, ignoring the frightened woman beside him as he peered through the sedan's rear window at the gray Alfa Romeo that was clearly trailing them.

"Stop, and let's take him," Malara said. He'd already retrieved an Uzi from under his seat and was ready to cock it.

"Not yet," Cortale replied. To Terranova, he added, "Drive on past these houses, along to where we choose left or right."

Via Solferino was a dead-end road that split before you reached its terminus, each segment leading to a different farm before it simply stopped. There was a point, just at the split, where neither of the two homes was close enough for residents to witness any action on the road or for a fool to get his courage up and try to intervene.

"The rest of you," Cortale said, "be ready."

Terranova reached beneath the driver's seat, took out a *lupara,* the classic sawed-off shotgun and set it beside him. Aiello drew a Beretta Cougar from its shoulder holster, easing back the slide an inch or so to make sure he had a live round in the pipe.

Cortale, for his part, preferred a larger weapon. Leaning

forward, he released a hidden catch that, in turn, released a sort of flap in the seat in front of him. Once opened, it revealed an AKS-74U assault rifle, the Kalashnikov carbine with shortened barrel and folding stock, which still retained the full firepower of its parent AK-74. Cortale lifted out the little man-shredder, retrieved two extra magazines, then closed the hidden hatch. He turned again and saw the Alfa still behind them, hanging back three hundred yards or so but matching every twist and turn they made.

"Who is it?" the woman asked.

"How should I know?"

"Maybe someone Aldo sent to help us," Terranova offered, though he didn't sound convinced.

"What help?" Malara challenged him. "We don't need any help."

To which the driver simply shrugged.

"More likely, someone from the Gugliero family," Aiello said with an expression like he had a bad taste in his mouth.

"It's possible," Cortale granted.

There'd been trouble off and on for two years now between the Magolino family and Nikola Gugliero's clan from Botricello. Gugliero's soldiers had begun to poach on Magolino turf, trying to horn in on the drug trade and the gambling. No blood had been spilled, but tense negotiations had not managed to resolve the problem, either. It was possible that Gugliero had his people shadowing Adamo and the other Magolino officers, looking for ways to undercut them and watching for a chance to bring them down.

"Those assholes need a lesson," said Malara. "We're the ones to let them have it."

"Only one man in the car that I can see," Terranova reported.

"*Merda.* The rest are likely hiding in the trunk," Aiello said.

"Quiet!" Cortale ordered. "Let me think."

He had a problem. Killing came easy to Cortale, as to

all of them, but first he needed some idea of who the target was. Blasting a member of the Gugliero family, although it might be satisfying, could provoke a war. Likewise, if they were being followed by a cop, killing him might touch off a vendetta from the law. And finally, if they were wrong about the Alfa's driver—if, for instance, he was simply traveling to one of the last homes on Via Solferino—the murder of an innocent civilian could provoke investigation of their presence in the area.

"Well?" Malara prodded him.

"Dino," Cortale said, "when you reach the fork, stop short and block the road. We'll see what this bastard wants and then decide what we should do with him."

BOLAN HAD CHECKED the Alfa's GPS and knew he was running out of road. Three-quarters of a mile ahead, the track they were following divided, one part going north a hundred yards or so before it hooked hard right and came to a dead end. The other traveled half as far, due south, before it ended in a cul-de-sac. Whichever fork the four *'ndrang-hetisti* chose, there'd be no turning back.

Which made him wonder, once again, if they'd spotted him.

The Alfa would be difficult to miss, but with the lead vehicle's tinted windows, Bolan couldn't tell if they were watching him or not.

Next question: Was the side road they were following the route his targets meant to take, or was Bolan being led into a trap? Did it make any difference? Whatever happened in the next few minutes, Bolan's goal remained the same. Eliminate the goons and liberate their prisoner.

He left the big Beretta in its holster. Placing it beside him on the vacant seat would make it handy, but a sudden stop could also send it spinning out of reach. Why risk it, when the piece was close enough to draw and fire within

a second? As for Bolan's other guns, they lay behind the
driver's seat in duffel bags, secure but reachable.

And if his targets had a trap in mind, they might be
needed any moment now.

The black sedan ahead of him was slowing, no brake
lights, the driver lifting off the accelerator as he neared the
fork in the road. Bolan followed suit, not closing in as yet,
giving the 'Ndrangheta wheelman time to make his choice.
Ahead of them, he saw more open fields and orchards and
houses in the middle distance, left and right.

The dwellings gave him pause. If this had been the hit
team's destination from the start, there would likely be
more men, more guns, waiting at whichever house they
pulled up to. Conversely, if this was a trap, they could be
drawing innocents into the line of fire. It was a problem
either way, but one he'd have to work around. Retreating
now, leaving the woman to her fate, was not an option.

He was considering a run-up toward the lead car, something that would force their hand, when the sedan stopped
short and turned to block both lanes. Its doors flew open
and disgorged four men with guns in hand. They left the
woman in the backseat, pale face peering out at him with
frightened eyes.

The four *'ndranghetisti* fanned out in a skirmish line,
advancing toward the Alfa like gunfighters in a spaghetti
western. Bolan weighed his options, drawing the Beretta
93R from its holster, then thumbing the selector switch to
go with 3-round bursts. Its magazine held twenty rounds,
with one more in the chamber, and he trusted that would
be enough.

But first, a little something to disorient the enemy.

He gunned the Alfa's engine, charging toward the stag-
gered line of gunmen in his path. Their faces told him
they'd expected something else—perhaps that he'd retreat
or step out of the Giulietta with his hands raised in surrender. What they hadn't counted on was some two thousand

pounds of steel accelerating toward them with a hungry snarl.

They scattered, running for their lives. One slower—maybe more courageous—than the rest, stood his ground just long enough to rake the Alfa with a burst of automatic fire. Bolan ducked below the dash, pebbles of glass raining over him, and held his charger steady on its course. A solid *thump* denoted impact, then the tardy goon was airborne, glimpsed in passing as he soared over the car and fell somewhere behind it.

Braking short of contact with the lead car, Bolan cranked his steering wheel hard left and veered off pavement toward the nearest cultivated field. A moment later, he was out and moving, ducking bullets as the three men who were still upright laid down a screen of fire.

CORTALE SAW THE speeding car clip Terranova, launching him into a somersault that carried him over the Alfa Romeo and dropped him behind it. He landed with an ugly *crunch* on the pavement. From his cries and jerky movements, Terranova clearly was not dead, but there was no time to assist him now—Cortale was busy hammering the gray car with a burst from his Kalashnikov.

Where was the driver, damn it? The man was down below his line of fire, so Cortale ripped another burst across the left-hand doors and hoped the bullets reached him, while the Alfa left the roadway, plowing into a nearby field. He strafed the car with another burst, Malara and Aiello joining in, before a rising cloud of dust obscured the vehicle.

Somewhere amid that cloud, the driver rolled out of his seat and started firing back. He had an automatic weapon, rattling 3-round bursts that sounded like 9 mm rounds. Cortale ducked and veered to his left, putting the bullet-punctured Alfa between himself and whoever it was that seemed intent on killing him.

And why?

He had no time to think about that, only to flank the son of a whore and kill him before they lost any more men. If they couldn't—

The woman!

Remembering her in the midst of chaos, Cortale risked a glance toward his sedan, its four doors standing open, and saw no one left inside. Snarling obscenities, he almost went to look for her but realized he couldn't take that risk. The woman mattered less now than disposing of their enemy.

And if she got away? What then?

Cortale could not bear to think about it. He was focused on surviving in the moment. He would deal with Aldo in his turn, explain as best he could, and—

To his right, Malara cursed and ripped an empty magazine out of his Uzi's pistol grip, fumbling inside his jacket for another. He retrieved it and was about to load the little submachine gun when a triple-tap from their opponent ripped into Malara's left shoulder and spun him like a ballerina through an awkward pirouette. Malara sat down hard, a red mist from his wound painting his startled face, trying to raise the SMG one-handed from his lap.

Cortale fired another long burst at the bastard who was slaughtering his men, and then his own damned magazine was empty. Running for the nearest cover, a weed-choked roadside ditch, he dived headlong into its dusty sanctuary, the Kalashnikov digging into his ribs. Cortale rolled onto his back, feeling the seconds slip away as he released the empty magazine, discarded it, replaced it, and then jacked a round into the carbine's chamber.

Ready!

But for what?

Out in the open, Ruggiero Aielo was stalking their prey, shouting taunts and insults to provoke him. Terranova and Malara were still alive, after a fashion, though Cortale could not count on either one of them right now. The woman could be anywhere, escaping while he lay there in the dirt, his Armani suit a filthy mess of dust and briars.

"Curse her rotten soul," he muttered.

And what about the neighbors? They had telephones, no doubt, but would they risk a call to the authorities? Speaking to the police was dangerous in Italy, but some high-minded citizens still clung to what they thought of as their civic duty. If the cops turned up with the firefight still in progress, Cortale was prepared to kill them, too.

Why not? They should know better than to interfere. If they hadn't learned that much from history, or on the job, they were too stupid to survive.

Cortale raised his head, risking a glance across the roadway, looking for his enemy. Instead, he saw Malara rising slowly, painfully, using his Uzi as a prop while struggling to his feet, blood drizzling on the pavement from his wounds. Behind him, fifty feet or so away, Terranova was crawling toward their car, dragging one limp and twisted leg behind him, teeth clenched in a snarl of agony. Aiello was still hunting, edging closer to the Alfa, his slacks now pale with dust from the knees down. He'd stopped calling to their enemy and clutched his pistol in a good two-handed grip, ready to fire at the first glimpse of movement.

Suddenly embarrassed, Cortale rolled out of the ditch and rose, moving to join his men.

THE FOUR 'NDRANGHETISTI were legitimate tough guys; Bolan conceded that. One shot, another knocked ass over teakettle at fifty miles per hour, and they both had fight left in them yet. The other two were coming on as if they didn't have a worry in the world: no fear of bullets, witnesses, police, nothing. Some mobsters he had known—and killed— would have been running for their lives by now, but the Magolino goons were going out with style.

So let them go.

First, Bolan focused on the soldier who'd been stalking

him, trying to lure him out with insults, firing random shots to cover his approach. That method had a fatal flaw, which the mobster discovered when the slide locked open on his pistol's empty chamber and he had to swap magazines out in the open, with nowhere to hide.

Bolan rose and hit him with a 3-round burst at center mass, knocking him backward. This one was a solid kill, no doubt about it from the thrashing of his legs, then the stillness as he lay sprawled on his back.

And that left three.

The other one still fit to fight was coming hard at Bolan, firing from the hip with a Kalashnikov. No one who'd ever had an AK fired in their direction could mistake its sound or minimize the danger of exposure to its raking fire. Bolan went down as if he'd been hit, lay prone and fired from that position, knowing he might not score a fatal shot but doing what he could with what he had.

Two of his three rounds ripped into the shooter's pelvis, drilling guts and shattering the heavy bone to break him down. Legs folded, and the screaming mobster slumped into his line of fire to take the next burst through his jaw and throat, face shattered, brain stem severed as he dropped.

Two down and out.

Bolan had fired five bursts, which meant he still had six rounds left to go. Rising, he saw the gunner he'd wounded moments earlier trying to raise an Uzi with his one functioning hand. Barely functioning, apparently, because it wasn't working out for him. The skinny gangster saw death coming, cursed it and went down as Bolan shot him in the chest.

Last up, the man who wasn't quick enough to dodge his Alfa at the start of their engagement, crawling like a crippled beetle on the blacktop. Bolan sent him mercy from a range of thirty feet and watched him slump facedown, no longer dangerous to anyone.

Reloading on the move, Bolan surveyed the battleground and couldn't see the woman. She'd escaped, and he could let it go at that, if it was what she wanted. He retreated to the bullet-riddled Alfa, knew it wasn't going anywhere and got his bags out of the car. Bolan turned back to the un-damaged black sedan still idling where its passengers had bailed to start the firefight.

"I'm going now," he called out, speaking in Italian. "Good luck."

He made it to the mobsters' car and had stowed his guns and settled in the driver's seat before she called out to him from behind a bristling roadside hedge. "Please wait!"

He waited while she made her cautious way to the sedan and peered in at him through a window. Overcoming fear at last, she asked, "Can you take me somewhere?"

Bolan holstered the Beretta as he said, "All right. Get in."

Catanzaro

ALDO ADAMO LISTENED to the caller's words, feeling his stomach clench. "What do you mean, you haven't seen them yet?" he asked.

"Just what I said," his man aboard the *Mare Strega* answered. "There's no sign of them, and Cortale hasn't called."

"They should have been there—" Aldo studied his Movado TR90 watch, scowling "—almost an hour ago."

"It's why I'm calling."

"All right. Wait there. I'll call you back."

Adamo cut the link and tried Cortale's cell phone, wait-ing through five rings before it went to voice mail. Know-ing that his number must have been displayed on Cortale's phone and that his soldier was not fool enough to miss the call deliberately, Aldo switched his phone off without leav-ing a message.

Something was wrong.

Adamo began to consider reasons why his people had not reached the boat. The first that came to mind was logical enough: they might have stopped somewhere along the way to play a little with the woman. He had not forbidden it, specifically, but Cortale should have been intelligent enough to do his business with her after they were all safely aboard the *Mare Strega,* out at sea. They would have privacy and all the time they needed.

But even if his soldiers had been stupid and had stopped along the highway leading south, Cortale would not turn off his phone or dodge a call from his superior. A *santista,* Cortale was on call around the clock. His time—indeed, his very life—was not his own.

Adamo's cell phone chirped at him, a soft sound, but it almost made him drop the instrument. Recovering, he answered on the second ring. "Hello?"

"Signore Adamo? This is Lieutenant Albanesi."

One of their men within the *Guardia di Finanza,* Albanesi never called unless there was some trouble in the offing—an indictment, for example, or a raid pending against some Magolino enterprise.

"Yes, Lieutenant. How may I assist you?" Aldo was going through the motions, as if they were simply friends and he was there to serve the fat little policeman.

"I'm afraid I have bad news," Albanesi said. "We have found four of your men outside Le Croci. They're dead."

"Dead? All four?"

"Regrettably. Yes, sir."

"What happened?"

"They were shot. It also seems that one of them was struck by a vehicle."

Adamo knew he must be careful with his next question. "Were they alone?"

"Yes," the officer confirmed. "Were you…expecting someone else?"

"No, no. I only thought, if there was shooting…"

"Ah, of course. They did return fire, but we've found no evidence so far that it accomplished anything. I wonder, sir, if you could say what sort of car they had?"

"Their car?" Adamo had to think about it for a moment, thrown off base by Albanesi's unexpected question. "It was a black Lancia Delta."

"And would you know the number of its license plate by any chance?"

"I couldn't say. It's registered commercially," Adamo answered. "To our winery, if I am not mistaken."

"Never mind," the lieutenant said. "I can check that myself."

"Why do you ask about the car?" Adamo pressed him.

"Ah. Because we found one at the scene, damaged by gunfire. It's a rental, from the airport at Lamezia Terme. It was hired out today, in fact, to someone named…um… Scott Parker. Is that name familiar to you, sir?"

"It is not," Adamo said. But it will be, he thought.

"An American, it appears, if we may trust his operator's license and the credit card he used to hire the car. We will be tracing both."

"Of course. Please keep me informed of any progress, and advise me when the bodies may be claimed for burial. Their families…"

"Under the circumstances," Albanesi said, "I'm afraid the magistrate will certainly demand autopsies. The delay in their release may be substantial."

"Do the best you can," Adamo said. "Your efforts are appreciated, Lieutenant."

Meaning that he owed the little troll another envelope of cash, with more to come if Albanesi could identify the killer and deliver him to the family.

But the main headache for Adamo now was the missing woman.

A headache he was about to share with his *padrino*.

Bracing for the storm to come, Adamo made the call.

4

"I need to ditch this car," Bolan informed his silent passenger. "As soon as possible."

"Of course." She answered dully, as if they were discussing the weather.

The police would find his rental car sometime within the hour, if they weren't already at the shooting scene. That meant they'd trace it to the airport and discover his I.D. An all-points bulletin was sure to follow, with a photocopy of his driver's license and a tight watch on his credit card in Scott Parker's name.

Bad news, but he was not prepared to call it a catastrophe.

The I.D. was disposable. Once he'd placed a call to Hal, inquiries into Scott Parker would collide with cold stone walls, all record of the man erased, leaving police—and anybody else who tried to trace him in the States—without a clue. As far as money went, he had enough on hand to see his mission through, and he could always pick up more by ripping off the 'Ndrangheta.

But his enemies would be looking for the car he'd borrowed. Whether they passed on its description to the cops or not, all eyes beholden to the syndicate would be wide open, watching for the black Lancia Delta.

Too bad, Bolan thought. It was a nice ride, but every minute he spent behind its wheel brought him closer to danger. Losing the car in Catanzaro shouldn't be a problem, but his best bet for a quick replacement was the long-term parking lot at the same airport where he'd rented the Alfa Romeo. Maybe he could put the woman on a flight out of Calabria at the same time.

"You saved my life," the woman said, as if the thought had just occurred to her.

"Happy to do it," Bolan replied.

"But why?"

"Why not?"

She hesitated. "Are you…'ndranghetisto?"

"No," Bolan said. "Not even close."

She tried again. "Police?"

"I'm strictly unofficial," he said. She looked confused. "You are not Italian."

"No."

" American, I believe."

"Does it matter?" Bolan asked.

"No, I suppose not. I simply want to understand."

"I saw an opportunity to help and took it. Let it go at that."

"What happens now?"

"First, I find another set of wheels, and then I make arrangements that will keep you safe."

That brought a bitter laugh. "Where on Earth will I ever be safe?"

"I have some friends. They'll think of something."

"Oh, yes. That's what they told my brother. Now he's dead and I am hunted like an animal."

"Your brother?"

"Rinaldo," she answered. "Rinaldo Natale."

"I've heard of him," Bolan said. "He was—"

"An informant, yes. He brought shame onto all of us."

"And you were being punished for it."

Bolan knew the ground rules of a classic vendetta. No survivors could be tolerated.

"Not only me," she replied. "My mother, aunts and uncles, cousins. Everyone. Gianni will not rest while any of them are alive."

"Gianni Magolino."

She was staring at him now, eyes narrowed. "You know of him?"

He rolled the dice. "I'm here because of him. Because he killed your brother in the States."

"I asked if you are police," she said, her tone accusatory.

"And I'm not," Bolan assured her.

"What, then?"

"Someone who solves problems when the law breaks down."

"What will you do with me?"

"I told you. Find someplace where you'll be safe."

"There's no such place in Italy. No such place in the world."

"You'd be surprised."

She laughed at that. "I'll be surprised if I wake up alive tomorrow, *Signor*… What should I call you?"

"Scott Parker," Bolan said. At least for now, he thought.

"And I am Mariana."

"Pleased to meet you."

"How will you save me then?" she asked.

"First thing, we find new wheels. Then I need to make a call."

Le Croci

CAPTAIN NICOLA BASILE stepped out of his Fiat Bravo, surveying the crime scene on Via Solferino. Off to his left, a bullet-riddled Alfa Romeo sat in a farmer's field. The pavement before him was bloodstained, with police trying to step around the evidence while taking measurements and photographs. Basile frowned as he saw Lieutenant Carlo Albanesi approaching, face cracked by a smile.

"Captain, you're here."

"Where else should I be, Lieutenant?"

Albanesi blinked at him. "I simply meant—"

"I understand four dead *'ndranghetisti*. True?"

Albanesi took the interruption in stride. "That is correct."

"Their names?"

Albanesi took a notebook from his pocket and consulted it. "Ruggiero Aiello, Gitano Malara, Fausto Cortale and Dino Terranova."

"So, the Magolino family," Basile said. "And no one else?"

"No one."

"Their car?" Basile nodded toward the Alfa in the field.

"No, sir. We think theirs was stolen. This one is an airport rental, hired by an American." Albanesi's eyes went back to the notebook. "A Scott Parker of Baltimore. Examination of flight records is proceeding at Lamezia Terme as we speak."

Basile would have praised most any other officer for that report, but he could not bring himself to congratulate Albanesi. The lieutenant was a dirty cop—reputed to be a bagman for the 'Ndrangheta. He'd been untouchable so far because the cash he collected flowed to higher-ranking officers within the *Guardia di Finanza*. Even so, Basile—who had never touched a bribe in twenty-seven years—refused to treat him with respect and was constantly on watch for ways to bring him down.

"What about the dead men's vehicle?" Basile asked.

"We're looking into it," Albanesi said. "No description yet."

"Have you asked Gianni Magolino?"

Yet another blink from Albanesi as he answered, "No. Why would I?"

Smiling vaguely to himself, Basile answered, "Why?

To question him about his poor *santisti,* cut down in their prime. Why else?"

"I thought it more important to get after the American," Albanesi said. "And I did not wish to trespass on your territory."

"Mine?"

The fat lieutenant shrugged. "A man of Magolino's stature. Surely he deserved a captain, eh?"

"Perhaps you're right, Lieutenant. Why insult him by sending a lackey?"

Albanesi stiffened, color rising in his jowls, but whatever tart response had come to mind, he wisely kept it to himself.

Basile eyed the cartridge casings scattered around the scene and said, "The dead were armed, I take it?"

Albanesi nodded silently, still simmering.

"With automatic weapons, it appears."

"An Uzi, a Kalashnikov, some pistols."

"Good. Perhaps *Signore* Magolino can explain where his employees got that kind of hardware in Calabria."

A scornful snort. "You think he'll tell you?"

"I hope not," Basile said.

He'd confused the fat lieutenant once again. Not difficult, but satisfying.

"You hope not?"

"When he refuses, or pleads ignorance, I may have grounds for a search warrant. Possession of unlicensed firearms is a serious offense. Distribution of such arms to others, much more so."

Albanesi shrugged, as if to say Basile was free to waste his time should he choose to. Both knew his application for a warrant might well be rejected by one of the several magistrates who banked on Magolino money for a posh retirement. In any case, Basile thought, the odds of finding Magolino personally in possession of illegal arms were slim to none.

But irritating the *padrino* was still a priceless exercise. Dangerous, certainly, but satisfying all the same.

When it came to dealing with the 'Ndrangheta, Basile was cautious but not terrified. That might come later, but he reckoned it was worth the risk. In the meantime, he would watch his back and keep his weapons close, prepared to go down fighting if it came to that.

"It seems you have the situation well in hand," he said, nearly gagging on the quasi-compliment. "I'll go now and give Magolino your regards."

As he retreated to his car and drove away, Basile was pleased to imagine Albanesi glaring after him.

Robert F. Kennedy Department of Justice Building, Washington, D.C.

HAL BROGNOLA'S MOBILE satellite phone was the smallest and lightest available, tipping the scale at a mere seven ounces. Its long, angular antenna contributed half of that weight and sometimes made Hal feel as if he were talking into the bowl of a meerschaum pipe.

With the sat phone, Hal could reach out to Stony Man or his operatives nearly anywhere on Earth. In fact, he refrained from calling agents in the field, except in dire emergencies where some bit of intelligence he possessed might help avert disaster. Otherwise, he thought it best to spare them needless interruptions when their focus meant the difference between survival and a grisly death.

And when the sat phone rang, Hal always felt a little chill that lifted the short hairs on his nape. Experience had taught him that calls rarely brought good news. More often, by a ratio of ninety-odd to one, the callers had some problem they were hoping Brognola could resolve by pulling strings in Washington, dispatching fresh supplies or reaching out to trusted contacts overseas. Hal didn't mind—that was his function, after all—but some days he sat dreading the phone's customized ringtone.

Days like today—and damn, there it was.

Hal snared it midway through the second ring, scrambler engaged. Wrong numbers could not reach his phone, in theory, but if they did, the caller would hear nothing but a shrill tone reminiscent of a fax line.

"Go," he said.

"It's me." Bolan, calling from Italy.

"How's it going?" Brognola asked.

"There's a wrinkle," Bolan said. "Make that two wrinkles."

"Oh?"

"First up, the witness from Shelter Island has a sister. I just met her. Magolino's boys were taking her for seafood."

"I suppose she's off the menu."

"Reservation canceled. Now, the thing is, she needs somewhere safe to go."

Brognola thought it through in seconds. "I won't get any traction here," he said, "unless she's got something to share."

"Like, say, an inside view from Magolino's headquarters?"

"Depends. If it connects to the indictment in Manhattan, she'd be useful. If it's all Calabrian, I doubt the prosecution will import her."

"I don't have any details for you yet," Bolan replied. "But while we're sorting that, I'd like to see if we can keep her breathing."

"And your thought is…"

"Are there any cops you trust in the neighborhood of Catanzaro? Someone who can stash her out of sight while I take care of business?"

That was tough. Hal knew a captain of the GDF who might be sympathetic to the lady's plight, but if he tied it to Bolan's blitz against the 'Ndrangheta, that could blow the deal sky-high, along with any hopes of collaboration down the road.

"It could be...sensitive," Brognola said.

"The story of my life," Bolan replied.

"This guy I know, he's arrow-straight. We've checked him seven ways from Sunday, and he's clean. Despite that, he's advanced on merit, through his record of arrests and solid cases. Mafiosi, terrorists, a couple psychos, take your pick."

"I'm waiting for the other shoe," Bolan said.

"Just this—he's by the book. I can't swear that he never cuts a corner, but he won't run off on any tangents helping you take Magolino down."

"Nobody's asking that," Bolan replied. "Just help a lady stay alive and maybe file some of those solid cases in the process."

"If there's anybody left to prosecute."

"There always is."

"Okay," Brognola said. "His name's Basile. Nicola Basile. Hang on for a second while I get his number for you."

Before he set the phone down, Hal's mind clicked and he asked Bolan, "What's the second wrinkle?"

"The police will have my rental car by now."

"Meaning your name and paperwork."

"Yes."

"Okay. Phone number first, and then I'll see what Stony Man can do about the rest."

Viale Alvaro Corrado, Catanzaro

"YOU HAVE DISAPPOINTED me severely," Gianni Magolino said.

Standing before his master's desk, Aldo Adamo realized there was no defense he could offer. He couldn't shift the blame onto his slaughtered soldiers. As the second in command, he'd been given an assignment and had failed to see it through. Whatever consequences might flow from that failure, they would fall on him.

"I understand," Aldo said. "The fault is mine, of course."

"Spare me self-righteous martyrdom," his godfather replied. "What do we know of this American who has interfered with our business?"

"Only his name and his address in the United States, if they are accurate."

"You doubt it?" Magolino asked.

"He is obviously a professional," Adamo answered. "Commonly, they travel with false papers, often multiple identities."

"You've started searching the hotels, of course."

"Yes. If he took a room, we'll find out where it was."

Adamo, for his part, had doubts about this Scott Parker checking into a hotel under the same name he'd used to hire a car.

"And at the airport?"

"We are still seeking the data on his reservation. The commercial carriers take time."

"And charter services?"

"None recognized his name or photograph."

"The name may change. But if we have his face…"

"Indeed, sir." But Adamo's tone betrayed him.

"Where's your confidence?" Magolino asked.

"What we have, *padrino,* is a photocopy of his driver's license from America. It's not the best, but one of my *santisti*—the computer man, whom you've met—tells me photographs on passports and the like may be manipulated."

"Explain."

"I do not understand it all myself," Adamo said. "He tells me you can take digital photos of a person, then 'adjust' them until they are similar but not the same. Distort the features slightly, or graft others from a different person's face. The new ones come out close enough to satisfy a passport check, for instance, but on close examination, they may just as easily be someone else entirely."

Magolino waved the scientific talk away. "I don't care what was done to any photograph. You have a name and a description. Find this bastard who made a mockery of us and bring him to me, alive, if possible. If not, bring me his head."

Adamo smiled at that.

"You won't forget our Mariana, eh?"

"Of course not, *padrino*."

"She can seriously damage each and every one of us. The taint of an informant is upon her. Do not let her speak to the authorities."

"No, sir."

But Magolino was not finished yet. "Your life is forfeit for today's disaster," he said. "This you know. Whether I choose to take it from you shall depend on how you deal with this unhappy situation. Solve it soon, my brother, and you'll find that much may be forgiven. If you fail…"

He said no more, but drew the index finger of his right hand slowly across his throat. Adamo got the message loud and clear.

Lamezia Terme International Airport

SWITCHING CARS WASN'T a problem. Bolan took a long-term parking ticket for the Lancia Delta and parked it between a panel van and a Fiat Sedici. He replaced it with a Fiat Panda, navy blue, whose cautious owner had left a spare key in a small magnetic box inside the right-rear wheel well. The parking ticket on the Panda's dash was one day old, suggesting Bolan would have a few more days, at least, before its rightful owner came to look for it. Leaving the lot, Bolan paid the tab and started back to Catanzaro, Mariana Natale slumped in the seat beside him, his weapons riding in back.

Bolan had heard her story—or at least the parts of it she felt like sharing with him. She'd been born into an 'Ndrangheta family, four generations of *santisti* and *vangeli* on her father's side. Her brother naturally went into the family business, leaving Mariana to consider whether she'd marry someone from the *cosche* and adopt a life of ease or possibly become a nun. The route she chose instead, playing the field with influential mobsters, nearly led her father to disown her, but he'd relented when Gianni Magolino took her as his mistress. Any further criticism was forbidden, and her father's death—an ambush by a gang of Camorra mobsters on a trip to Rome—had silenced him for good. The rest of Mariana's family still regarded her with thinly veiled distain, but they never managed to reject the gifts she bought for them with Magolino's money.

Her brother changed all that when he was busted by the DEA and chose to violate the code of silence rather than accept a prison term that would have put him back in circulation sometime in the next millennium. From that point on, the rest of the Natale family was forced to make a choice: deny the traitor and do everything within their power to destroy him, or prepare to share his fate. Now, with Rinaldo dead, it seemed Gianni Magolino had decided the rest of them should go, too.

"I got a name and number," he told Mariana on the short drive back to Catanzaro. "Someone who's supposed to be trustworthy."

"Ah. *Supposed* to be."

"I trust my source," he said. "Of course, we don't know till we try."

"And then what?"

"That depends on you. They'll probably want something in return for guaranteeing your security."

"Security!" she scoffed. "Rinaldo had security."

"Or I can drop you off somewhere in town, and you can take your chances. Your call."

"You don't care if I live or die?"

Emotional blackmail didn't work on Bolan. "If I didn't care," he said, "you'd still be back with Magolino's men. It doesn't mean I'm adopting you."

"You have a job to do," she said. "I understand, believe me." She turned to him, staring. "They'll kill you. Do you understand that?"

"They've been trying for a while," Bolan replied. "It isn't working out for them so far."

"You don't know Catanzaro. Anyone who does not serve the family is either ostracized or liquidated. You're a foreigner, a stranger. Just because you speak the language, more or less, does not mean you'll survive."

"Thanks for the vote of confidence," he said.

"I'm simply telling you the truth."

Bolan changed the subject. "I'll reach out to this new contact once we're back in town. You can speak to him yourself. If you decide to try it on your own instead, I'll take you anywhere you want to go, within a reasonable distance."

"So you wash your hands of me."

"I told you—"

"No adoption, right. But what about the rest of my family?"

She clearly meant her blood relations now, and not the 'Ndrangheta *cosche* whose godfather had decided she must die.

"Maybe they'll make a deal."

Her laugh was bitter, jagged. When it passed, she told him, "You know nothing of our ways."

He could have argued with her, told her he'd been dealing with oath-bound secret societies since one of them had killed most of *his* family, but what would be the point? The lady had escaped death, for the moment, and was feeling sorry for herself. Bolan had a war to fight in Catanzaro.

Starting any minute now.

5

Catanzaro

"This is a waste of time," Niccolo Gatti said. "We should be *doing* something."

Raf Dondini half turned toward him from the Maserati Quattroporte's shotgun seat and answered. "We're doing just what Aldo told us to. If that's a problem for you, take it up with him."

"Goddamn hotels," Gatti groused. "We've checked a dozen of them—"

"Five," Arturo Pino said.

"Whatever," Gatti told their driver. "No one has seen this damned American."

"We can say that when we've checked them all," Pino replied.

"How many more?"

"We got the shortest list," Pino informed him. "Twenty-eight to go."

"That will take all night!"

"Can't wait to see his little stripper," Mimmo Renni said, smiling.

"She's a dancer," Gatti muttered.

"A naked dancer."

"Shut it, eh?"

"Enough!" Dondini snapped. "You want to fight, wait till we're finished working."

His backseat soldiers lapsed into uneasy silence, Gatti glowered while Renni smiled, self-satisfied. They were like children sometimes, quarreling over trifles. It could be amusing under certain circumstances, but tonight their bickering was getting on Dondini's nerves. They had a job to do.

Two enemies. And not a sign of them, so far.

Dondini's orders had been simple—find the two of them, presumably together, and retrieve them, one way or another. His team was assigned to scour hotels on the southwest side of Catanzaro, and Dondini would complete that task without complaint, although he secretly agreed with Gatti that it was a waste of time.

Aldo had told them the American was some kind of professional. It stood to reason, then, that he wouldn't leave paper trails all over town. The rental car was one thing, maybe unavoidable if he was operating solo, but hotels were something else. Too many witnesses, particularly if he brought the woman back with him after he'd killed four men to free her.

The best thing Dondini could do right now was find the American and the woman. Although Don Magolino wanted them alive, Aldo had acknowledged that might not be possible. Accordingly, Dondini's team was armed to deal with any threat they might encounter: two Heckler & Koch MP5K submachine guns fitted with suppressors, a Franchi SPAS-15 semiautomatic shotgun and a Steyr AUG assault rifle, also with a suppressor. If they couldn't do the job with that hardware, each member of the team also carried at least one pistol and a knife for backup. Nothing was left to chance.

Dondini had known Cortale and the others who'd been killed that afternoon. They'd been his friends and his brothers in the Magolino family. Avenging them would be an honor, and the sooner it was done, the better, for the sake of all concerned.

"Where next?" Gatti asked.

Dondini checked his list, then said, "The Paradiso."

"That's five stars," Gatti said.

"So what?"

"This bastard's hiding out. Assuming he hasn't left the city, would he risk a five-star hotel?"

"He might think it's the last place anyone would look," Dondini said.

"Foolish," Gatti muttered.

"What was that?"

"Never mind."

"I'd like to be with Rocco's team when they find Mariana's mother," Renni said. "That should be fun."

"Not for the mother," Pino replied.

"Don Magolino should have killed them all the day Rinaldo sold us out," Gatti said.

"He had a soft spot for the girl," Pino suggested.

"Or a *hard* spot," Renni sniggered.

Dondini let them babble on. He found their disrespect for *il padrino* disconcerting, but their task was tiresome, and as Gatti said, they would be at it all night long—unless they caught a break. If they did, they would all be instant heroes to the family.

A little luck, he thought. That's all I need.

THE TELEPHONE RANG twice before a deep voice said, "Basile."

"You don't know me, Captain," Bolan said, "but a good friend tells me you're trustworthy."

"Who is this?"

"The one who stopped four of Gianni Magolino's boys from killing Mariana Natale."

After a momentary silence on the line, Basile said, "If that is true, we may have much to talk about."

"Maybe another time," Bolan replied. "Right now, the lady needs someplace where she can feel secure."

"Is she applying for immunity? Making an offer to co-operate with prosecutors?"

"None of that's for me to say," Bolan advised. "I need someone to take her off my hands and keep her safe while I go on about my business."

"Ah. And what, exactly, would that business be?" Basile asked.

"For your sake," Bolan said, "we'd better not get into that."

"Are you afraid of shocking me?"

"I'd hate to see you charged as an accomplice."

"So you have *illegal* plans."

Bolan ignored that. "Can you help the lady or not?"

"Facilities are available, but it requires a certain measure of discretion."

"As the marshals found out in New York," Bolan replied.

"Indeed. You're the American," Basile said. "May I call you Scott?"

"If it helps. That's not my name."

"I thought as much. You're a professional. May I inquire who sent you to Calabria?"

"Ask me no questions—"

"—and you tell no lies. I see. The arrangements for your friend may take some time."

"They need to be done as soon as possible. She's getting antsy."

Basile took another silent moment, then said, "I shall meet you. Do you know the Villa Margherita?"

"That's the garden right downtown."

"Correct. I will be waiting by the statue of Grimaldi in…one hour?"

"We can make that," Bolan answered, hoping Mariana would agree. "If this turns out to be a trap…"

"I'll be alone," Basile said. "You have my word."

"I'll take it…this time."

Bolan cut the link and turned to Mariana. She was watching him with a pinched expression.

"So it's arranged?" she asked.

"If you'll go through with it."

"And if I change my mind?"

"Same offer I made before."

"I cannot go to any member of my family," she said. "If they have not been rounded up, they will be watched."

"Maybe you can negotiate some kind of coverage for them," Bolan suggested.

Mariana shook her head. "Impossible. They were the first to turn against Rinaldo when he made the deal to testify. They have a code of honor, as I'm sure you understand. They will despise me, too, once I go into custody."

"Maybe they're safe then," Bolan said.

"Who knows? Gianni may decide to kill them all as a precaution. "If he does…"

She brushed her palms together, a dismissive gesture Bolan did not find convincing. She was putting up a front, being the mob girl who could take it all in stride, but bright tears were welling in her eyes.

"Where are we meeting this policeman?" she asked.

"At Villa Margherita," Bolan answered, "by the statue of Grimaldi." That one almost made him smile. Jack Grimaldi—Stony Man's top pilot—had been his wingman on campaigns that dated back to Bolan's private war against the Mafia.

"When?"

"One hour."

Mariana checked her watch. "It will be dark then. Still, it's a public place and lit after nightfall. Did you know it's close to Carabinieri headquarters?"

"That's news to me," Bolan admitted with a frown.

He knew that Italy's Carabinieri are the national military police, providing presidential security, guarding foreign embassies and collaborating with the *Guarda di Finanza* on anti-Mafia and anti-drug investigative task forces. Bolan didn't know how many Carabinieri were stationed in Catanzaro, but he guessed that handing Mariana off to Captain Basile in the shadow of their CP could be good or bad.

Good if it kept her safe.

Bad if Basile had an ambush waiting for them in the garden.

Would he be a friend or an enemy?

Bolan prepared to roll the dice.

Guardia di Finanza Headquarters

CAPTAIN BASILE DROPPED the telephone receiver back into its cradle, frowning at the instrument as if it had insulted him. In fact, his mind was racing in an effort to resolve the problem he had taken on, courtesy of the American known as Scott Parker.

There'd been no hesitation when Basile dropped the name, which verified what he'd already guessed. It was a cover, but for whom? For what?

This "Parker" might or might not be American, in fact. His nationality concerned Basile only inasmuch as it might help him to discern the stranger's motive and his future plan of action. He'd begun, or so he said, by saving Mariana Natale from what his fellow countrymen might call a one-way ride. Had that been part of his plan from the beginning or a mere coincidence?

I need someone to take her off my hands and keep her safe, he'd said, *while I go on about my business*. So, her rescue was not central to his plan, whatever that might be. It was no stretch of the imagination to decipher that he meant to harm the Magolino family—but what, exactly, did he have in mind?

Captain Basile had cooperated with Americans before. They reached out to him through their consulates in Naples or Palermo, introduced themselves and told him what their agencies—the FBI, DEA or ATF—hoped to accomplish in Calabria. Basile would negotiate terms, sometimes through his superiors, and help in any way Italian law and GDF procedure might allow.

In no case, ever, had Americans shown up and simply started shooting down 'ndranghetisti on the streets. It was outrageous—but it stirred Basile and made him wish he could lash out at his enemies sometimes, without restraint, to punish them as they deserved.

Enough of that, he thought. He was an agent of the government, bound by its laws and regulations. He did not cut corners, and his badge was not for sale to any criminal with a roll of euros in his pocket. But if he could hurt the Magolino cosche legally, perhaps by persuading Mariana Natale to talk, then it was worth a short walk from his office to collect from Villa Margherita.

However, the meeting might turn out to be a trap. Parker had warned him against any tricks, but what if that was just a ruse? Basile had made many enemies during his decades with the GDF, some in the Mafia and 'Ndrangheta, others in his own department. Honesty intimidated some police, and it shamed them with the knowledge of their own corruption. A few of those men were dangerous. Lieutenant Carlo Albanesi, for example, might not have the heart to pull a trigger personally, but Basile wagered that he wouldn't shrink from helping others do the dirty work.

Before leaving his desk, Captain Basile double-checked his sidearm. It was a Beretta 84BB, chambered in .380 ACP, with a double-stacked magazine holding thirteen rounds, plus one in the chamber. He had only fired the pistol once in self-defense, and that day had ended the life of a serial rapist who thought his knife beat a pistol.

Damned fool. And good riddance.

The killing had not troubled Basile any more than stepping on a scorpion, though he'd been forced to see a counselor and "share his feelings" in a session he'd found embarrassing. How should he feel, for taking out a psychopath who had abused at least a dozen women and who'd meant to gut him like a fish?

Relieved, of course. Pleased with a job well done.

Basile hoped there'd be no shooting around Villa Margherita. Self-preservation aside, he did not want to get mixed up with the Carabinieri if he could avoid it.

Keep it safe and simple. Bring the woman in alive, and see what happened next.

Siano, Calabria

PEPPINO LANZA RARELY watched the news channel on television, preferring Sportitalia, but tonight he found the broadcast vastly entertaining. Someone, bless them, had killed four soldiers from the Magolino *cosche* of the 'Ndrangheta and escaped unharmed. Police had nothing much to say about the shooting, which had happened in Le Croci, and Lanza hoped that meant they would not find the man or men responsible before they struck again.

His feelings toward the Magolino clan were understandable. As the local capo of a Mafia family based in Palermo, he stood at odds with the *'ndranghetisti* and naturally celebrated any harm that came to them. Gianni Magolino had tried to kill Lanza three times in the past eighteen months, which explained Lanza's present lodgings in Siano, a small town northeast of Catanzaro. It was an embarrassment, but Lanza's efforts to retaliate, so far, had been in vain.

The phone rang at his elbow, distracting him from the same view of bloody pavement he'd seen repeatedly since early evening. He was still enjoying it, of course. The sight of 'Ndrangheta blood never got old.

He grabbed the phone and answered. "*Sì.*"

"You've heard the news?" a strange voice asked in passable but obviously non-native Italian.

"I'm watching it right now," Lanza replied, frowning. "Who is this?"

"I'm a friend."

"I know all my friends by name," the mafioso said.

He was about to cut the link when the caller said, "I thought you'd want to know your life's in danger."

"What else is new?" Lanza asked.

"Gianni Magolino blames you for his loss this afternoon. He's planning to retaliate."

Now Lanza clutched the telephone more tightly, scowling at the television. He was on the verge of questioning this stranger when he caught himself. Suppose this was some trick by the authorities, a plan to see if Lanza would admit responsibility for killing Magolino's soldiers? Did they really think he was such a fool?

He replied, forcing a raspy chuckle as he spoke. "I don't know what you're smoking, but I wish I had some."

"Maybe it's a joke to you," the caller said, "but Magolino isn't laughing. Someone's on his way to visit you, for payback."

"For what?" Lanza demanded. "I've done nothing!"

An explosion rocked his house, shattering windows, rattling the dishes in his kitchen cabinets. As Lanza bolted from his chair, a rain of dust fell on his head and shoulders from the ceiling.

"See?" the caller asked him and was gone—a click, and then the dial tone buzzing in his ear.

Two of his soldiers reached the front room of the rented house ahead of Lanza, weapons in their hands, peering through windows where a ragged edge of broken glass remained. Lanza immediately recognized the acrid smell of high explosives.

"A grenade, I think," one of his men said. "They likely fired or threw it from the street, over the wall."

"They've gone now," the other said. "We should leave before the police get here."

"Pack up," Lanza commanded. "Quickly."

He obeyed his own instruction, retreating to the den where he'd been watching television moments earlier, before the taunting call. Before the blast.

Someone was playing games, and Lanza did not like it. Count this as the fourth attempt to kill him since he'd come to Catanzaro to trespass on 'Ndrangheta turf. Granted, it wasn't much of an attempt—a drive-by bombing that had injured no one—but the insult stung, and Lanza was determined to repay it.

What was it the caller said?

Payback.

He wondered if the man would call again. If so, Lanza would pay greater attention to his words, attempt to find out who he was and why he'd called with a warning about Gianni Magolino's plans.

Some kind of trick? Perhaps. But even so, there was a chance Lanza could turn it to his own advantage. In the meantime, he would rally all the troops available to him and lay plans of his own.

Payback, indeed.

DRIVING BACK TO CATANZARO, Bolan checked the rearview mirror for police cars and saw nothing to alarm him. Mariana, in the seat beside him, was beginning to relax a little after the attack on Don Peppino Lanza's house.

"You'll start a war, you know," she said.

"More of a sideshow," Bolan replied. "For cover."

"Gianni calls Lanza the little weasel," Mariana said. "He has worked with mafiosi many times but always from a distance, trading favors. When the Bevilacqua family sent Lanza from Palermo, camping on Gianni's doorstep, Gianni was furious. They've tried to kill each other time and time again."

"I'll try to help them get it right."

"I'm still not sure about this meeting," she said.

They were about twenty minutes out from Villa Margherita. Bolan had called Captain Basile from the outskirts of Siano on his way to Lanza's place, hoping they could meet the hour's deadline with some time to spare. A look around the park—and Carabinieri headquarters—would help him judge whether the meeting was a setup or legitimate.

If traffic slowed them down, he'd have to take his chances. Two lives would be on the line if it went sour—Mariana's and his own.

Arrest, for Bolan, would be tantamount to death in Catanzaro. No help would be coming from the States, and he assumed the 'Ndrangheta would arrange his execution in the lockup long before he'd come to trial. That outcome was a possibility on most of Bolan's missions, but he held to his self-imposed rule where police were concerned. Bolan would dodge and evade them by any available means, short of deadly force, but if it came down to a killing confrontation, he would not have blue blood on his hands.

"Give it a chance," Bolan suggested. "If it doesn't feel right, you can walk away."

"To what?" she asked.

"We've been over this."

"Leave Italy, I know. You make it sound so easy."

"Starting over's never easy," Bolan said, "but people do it every day."

"While being hunted by the 'Ndrangheta?"

"That's where you could use official help. Cooperate for relocation. You don't owe the Magolino family anything."

"That doesn't help. You're raised a certain way, believing certain things, and it's not easy to change. You know?"

He knew, all right. And when it came to loss, he understood in spades.

"It's worth a listen anyway," he said. "Ask questions. If the answers put you off, we'll walk."

Assuming that was possible.

Via Ferdinando Galiani carried them south from Siano to Via della Lacina, westbound, leading into Catanzaro. Bolan made good time until he hit the central maze of one-way streets and had to approach his destination from the north. The closer they came, the more tension he sensed from Mariana.

Passing by the park, he scanned for watchers on the street but couldn't pick out anyone who looked suspicious. Likewise, no uniforms were loitering around the scene, although that didn't mean Captain Basile hadn't stationed plainclothes officers where they could watch the meetup and intervene. Bolan considered sending Mariana to meet the cop alone, but Hal had never steered Bolan into a trap before.

Always a first time, said a small voice in the back of Bolan's mind. He ignored it.

As he found a parking place down range, Bolan asked Mariana, "Are you ready?"

"You'll be with me, yes?"

"I will."

"Good," she said after a moment's hesitation. "Then let's get it over with."

6

Villa Margherita, Catanzaro

Captain Nicola Basile walked from GDF headquarters to the garden that had been a tourist draw since 1881, entering its web of footpaths from Via Jannoni. He was a few minutes early and was second-guessing his decision to come alone as promised and picturing the different things that could go wrong.

The phone call might have been a ruse to draw him here, where he could be abducted or assassinated by some mobster. A second possibility: the call was legitimate, but 'ndranghetisti might trail the American and Mariana Natale, killing anyone they met to end the threat that she would turn informer. Finally, despite his own security precautions, there was still an outside chance that someone from the GDF had overheard his conversation with Scott Parker—walls and telephones alike had ears these days—and told the 'Ndrangheta about the meeting.

Time to retire, Basile thought, saddened that during his entire career he'd been forced to guard against corruption not only from the criminals he tried to put away, but also from within the agency he served.

Time to retire, indeed. But first, he had to make it through this night alive.

Basile found the bust of Bernardino Grimaldi without difficulty. He checked his watch. Five minutes. At the stroke of nine, he saw two figures moving toward him on the same path he'd followed to his lookout post. A man and woman, clearly, but Basile still did not relax. Others might be hiding in the shadows, and he'd known some lethal women in his time.

When they were close enough to speak in normal tones, Basile said, "Mr. Parker and Ms. Natale, I presume."

"Captain Basile?" the man asked.

"Indeed," Basile said. "Shall I show you my credentials?"

"We can skip that," Bolan told him. "Let's get down to business."

"Yes. The lady needs protection from her former, shall we say, associates?"

"You know her brother's dead."

"I heard this. Somewhere in New York, was it?"

"And Magolino has her marked. I barely got to her in time this afternoon."

"That was fortuitous," Basile said. "The outcome was, alas, unfortunate."

"Four fewer *'ndranghetisti,*" Bolan answered. "You can thank me later."

That almost provoked a smile, but Basile maintained his glum professional expression.

"If I were a private citizen, perhaps a journalist, I might sing your praises. As a law enforcement officer, however, I condemn your methods."

"Noted. Can we deal with Mariana now?"

Basile nodded. "Certainly. Normally, the GDF would give consideration to a person threatened by the 'Ndrangheta. When that person is a member of that brotherhood or a close associate of members, however, we require a bit more…incentive."

Parker's companion spoke for the first time. "I can tell

you things," she said. "About Gianni Magolino and the rest. I know enough to put them all in prison."

"That is an attractive prospect, I admit," Basile said. "Of course, your information must be verified. It also would be helpful if we had evidence supporting your account."

"What kind of evidence?" she asked.

Basile shrugged and rocked on his heels, hands in his trouser pockets. "Ledgers," he suggested. "Or directions to locations where we might find contraband, corpses, whatever may persuade a court."

"Would a schedule of drug deliveries suffice?"

"If accurate, it would be very helpful."

Now she frowned. "Because I escaped, they may change dates and times."

Basile sighed. "In which case—"

"But I know the warehouse where Gianni keeps his product."

"Ah." Basile turned to Parker. "If this proves true, I'm certain we can strike a deal."

"With full security," Bolan said. Telling him, not asking.

"On my honor."

"Then I'm out of here," the American replied.

"Before you go…might I convince you to abstain from any further bloodshed in Calabria?"

"Sorry," the tall man said and let it go at that.

"In which case," Basile said, "I shall hope we do not meet again."

"Likewise." And he was gone.

BOLAN LEFT MARIANA and the captain, fairly certain he could trust Basile but less convinced about the rest of his department and the overall bureaucracy he served. Corruption was the grease that kept most government machinery working, though it sometimes clogged the system. In Italy, the problem was endemic, but many servants of the state did not consider it an issue.

It was simply part of life.

Now that Mariana was safe, Bolan could pick up where he'd been interrupted, starting with the hit list he'd compiled in transit from D.C.

Aldo Adamo's office would be closed by now, and Adamo himself was presumably engaged in hunting "Scott Parker." That would take him nowhere, and although his access to a touched-up photograph of "Parker" was unfortunate, it had no impact on Bolan's game plan.

When you want to hurt a mobster, hit him in the wallet. The economic lifeblood of the 'Ndrangheta flowed from human vice and weakness: drugs, gambling, debt and prostitution. All of those were cracks in the cartel's façade, where Bolan had an opportunity to drive his wedges deep.

He would begin with gambling. Slot machines, roulette, dice games and other common forms of casino gambling were ripe for exploitation by the mob.

The place he had in mind was a nightclub called *La Fiamma*—The Flame—that included a full-scale casino upstairs. Access to the casino was via invitation only, but the Executioner thought he could find a way inside without much difficulty.

Gianni Magolino's *'ndranghetisti,* however, might have a hard night coming up.

Luck of the draw, Bolan thought as he motored toward his target, leaving Villa Margherita in his rearview mirror.

Simeri Crichi, Calabria

DON PEPPINO LANZA reviewed his troops like a general preparing for battle—which, in fact, was close.

At best, he was a captain in the larger Bevilacqua family, and his "army" wasn't much to look at either. Twenty-seven men, all told, more like a platoon in the real world, but he would trust any one of these men with his life.

To a point.

Beyond that, in the best tradition of a fractured under-world, it was every man for himself.

Lanza's soldiers were a motley group, all the more so for having been summoned at such short notice. Still, they had shown up as ordered, armed and more or less ready for battle, with no one complaining. If spirit counted for anything, Lanza would match them against any force in the world.

And they were well armed. Their invasion of Magolino territory, ordered by Don Alessandro Bevilacqua himself, had been a not-so-subtle act of war and thus required a show of force. Each man carried an automatic weapon, mostly stolen military arms: Beretta AR90 rifles or the newer ARX-160 and a few Kalashnikovs. They also had a handful of submachine guns, including two Uzis, a Spectre M4, and a Beretta M12. In addition to those weapons, each soldier was armed with a pistol or two and assorted other toys, including grenades, garrotes and stilettos. Every man had brought all the ammunition he possessed, prepared to fight until the last round had been fired.

In other circumstances, Lanza would have been satisfied. Yet...

He had retreated to the town of Simeri Crichi, northeast of Catanzaro, where the Bevilacqua *coche* owned more property. With any luck, his small force would be unmolested until he forged a plan for retaliation. Don Bevilacqua had already learned of the latest insult to his family's honor and had made it plain that payback was required. Each soldier in the field must do his part.

And for Lanza's personal reputation, there was no time to waste. He had received criticism already for his failure to punish Gianni Magolino for the early attempts on his life. Their back-and-forth skirmishing was a topic of some discussion—not to say derision—among his brothers in Palermo. He had survived three near misses before tonight's explosion, and the best he'd offered in return was the drive-by execution of Gianni Magolino's main accountant.

A lousy bookkeeper.

It was embarrassing, and Lanza knew if he ever hoped for a promotion in the family—actually, if he simply wanted to survive—he must do something more. Don Bevilacqua had been explicit on the telephone tonight. This was his final chance. If he did not succeed, the family expected him to die in the attempt, expunging the dishonor with his blood.

Lanza, of course, preferred survival.

After a quick examination of his soldiers and their weapons, Lanza briefed them on the bombing of his rented house. By then they'd heard the news in one form or another, likely garbled, but his speech was meant to motivate them for the coming battle. All of them were loyal—to the family, if not to him specifically—but their *padrino's* do-or-die commandment was the final, surefire motivator.

Any man who let the *cosche* down should not expect to live.

"Now, men," he finished strong, "these Magolino scum would happily destroy us. Each and every one of you is marked, the same as I am. They hate you, and would steal the bread out of your mouths if we permit it. Shall we?"

Most of them responded with a rousing "No!" A few added profanities to emphasize their defiance. Three or four of them stood silent, grim-faced, hands white-knuckled where they clutched their weapons. Lanza took that as a sign of anger, not fear. Cowards did not survive long in the Bevilacqua family.

"Three of you will stay with me," he said. "The rest will be divided into four-man teams for hunting. Take the maps assigned to you and strike the targets you find marked. Destroy each one in turn, and leave none of our adversaries standing. The whole family depends on us to vindicate their honor. Are you with me?"

This time, all of them responded with a shouted "*Sì*" that filled the parlor of his rented home. Lanza picked out the three who would remain with him, then left the other twenty-four to form their teams as they saw fit.

Gianni Magolino had more soldiers. In Catanzaro proper, Magolino had at least a dozen for each of Lanza's men, with more dispersed throughout the countryside, but Lanza would have bet that none were superior. In fact, he *was* about to bet precisely that.

In this game, he would bet his life.

La Fiamma, Via Francesco Crispi, Catanzaro

THE FLAME WAS burning bright when Bolan made his drive-by. He found a nice dark place to park the Fiat Panda and took stock of his gear before he left the yard.

His normal M.O. was to be prepared for anything. In this case, that meant dressing well to pass inspection at the club's front door but packing enough heat to carry out his mission once he got inside. Bolan had brought the Spectre M4 SMG. With its stock folded, and minus the suppressor, it fit nicely beneath his right arm on a shoulder sling. Two extra casket magazines in each of Bolan's outer pockets balanced out the coat while giving him two hundred spare rounds.

Arriving on the nightclub's doorstep, he was casually vetted by a husky bouncer and admitted to the ground floor after payment of a modest cover charge. A sign inside the lobby warned him of a two-drink minimum, but Bolan didn't let it slow him.

The hostess who arrived to seat him frowned when Bolan told her he was headed for the second floor. "Do you have an invitation?" she asked.

"Right here," Bolan said, drawing back the right side of his coat. She gave a little gasp but didn't argue as he steered her toward the stairs off to their left.

Another guard was waiting there, standing behind a velvet rope that drooped across the bottom of the staircase.

Magolino's watchdog frowned at their approach, raising one eyebrow at the hostess as he asked, "Who is this?"

Before the hostess could reply, Bolan showed him the Spectre, stubby muzzle pressed against the mobster's rock-hard abs. Knowing his six-pack wasn't bulletproof, the soldier scowled but offered no resistance as his pistol was removed and deposited into one of Bolan's pockets.

"Lead the way," Bolan commanded, staying one step back as his two hostages proceeded up the stairs. When they had almost reached the second-story landing, yet another guard appeared and asked, "What the hell is going on?"

Bolan showed him, blasting a 3-round burst through lookout number one that sprayed his pal with blood, then triggering a second that erased the shocked look from his crimson-spattered face. The hostess screamed and folded, dropping to all fours. Bolan left her where she was and swept past the two fresh corpses into the casino.

Whether the players had missed the gunfire or mistook it for some kind of racket from the bank of slot machines, Bolan would never know. He removed any doubt as soon as he cleared the threshold and triggered a burst into the ceiling that released a rain of shattered glass and phosphorus over one of the roulette tables.

That set the gamblers scampering for any exit they could find as two more guards rushed forward, drawing pistols from beneath their blazers. Bolan dropped each one in turn, then scanned the room for any other challengers before he went to work on shutting down the place.

It wasn't difficult. A frag grenade dropped in the middle of the room would set off fire alarms and bring authorities with sirens screaming, but he took a moment first to sweep a couple of the nearest tables, scooping up as many euros as the inner pockets of his long coat would accommodate. It never hurt to supplement his war chest.

When he had harvested a hundred grand or so, he

palmed the OD/82-SE grenade, released its pin and left the bomb sizzling away as he headed back downstairs. The blast came seconds later, followed by an alarm blaring from hidden speakers, emptying the bar and dining room downstairs.

Bolan followed The Flame's retreating customers into the night, bound for his next stop on the hellfire trail.

Guardia di Finanza Headquarters

LIEUTENANT CARLO ALBANESI put the cell phone to his ear then instantly regretted it as shouted curses made him wince. He rose and rushed to close his office door, waiting until Aldo Adamo paused to draw a breath before speaking.

"Please, sir, if I may suggest—"

"Shut up and listen!"

Albanesi closed his mouth.

"You've heard from *La Fiamma,* I suppose?" Adamo asked.

Heard from a flame? The question puzzled Albanesi until his thoughts cleared and he recognized the name of Magolino's main casino. "What about it?" he replied.

"What about it? Are you trying to be humorous?"

"No, sir. If you would kindly—"

"Idiot! It's been raided and ransacked, four men killed."

"By the police? Surely, I would have heard—"

"Not the police. One man shooting my people and setting off explosives. Are you saying you've heard nothing?"

"No, I swear!" Albanesi's mind was racing, leaving his thoughts a tangle. "Perhaps the fire brigade has not called for assistance yet?"

"You're asking me? I pay you well to know these things!"

"I understand, sir. I shall make inquiries and—"

"Wait! I'm not finished."

"There's more?"

"Mariana Natale. I want her returned to me," Adamo said.

"Yes, sir. But I—"

"For what I pay you, I expect results, Lieutenant, not excuses."

"Certainly, but—"

"If she comes into your hands—by which I mean official hands of any kind—you will inform me instantly and take steps to secure her for me. Yes?"

Albanesi felt a catch in his throat as he replied, "Of course, sir."

"If you fail me, I shall have to reconsider your employment status. Your longevity may well be jeopardized."

"I understand completely, sir." Cold sweat had broken out on Albanesi's face. "But if she does not come to the authorities—"

"Then you must help me find her elsewhere. You are a detective, are you not?"

"Well—"

"Do your damn job!"

"Yes, sir!"

He would not attempt to correct Adamo's misconception of a poor lieutenant's normal duties. Those went out the window when a leader of the 'Ndrangheta called, reminding Albanesi that he could be crushed like any other insect if his masters give the order.

Adamo had signed off without a good-bye, and Albanesi cradled the telephone receiver as if fearing it might explode. He felt lightheaded, and his stomach churned from hearing both his life and livelihood threatened in no uncertain terms. He cursed Adamo, now that he was safe from being heard, but the rejoinder only made him feel more impotent.

Action would save him. Nothing else would do.

First, he must find out what had happened at The Flame and whether any witnesses were willing to talk. One man taking on the 'Ndrangheta? The idea struck Albanesi as preposterous until he thought about the massacre outside Le Croci and remembered Scott Parker. The American.

Could it be? Who else would tackle such a risky job alone?

Don't leap to a conclusion, Albanesi thought, but he was there already. Reaching for the phone once more, he thought about the other task Adamo had assigned to him and wondered whether it was even feasible.

He'd never met Mariana Natale. Would not, in fact, have recognized her if she walked into his office and sat down at his desk. But now she threatened his existence. Was it possible to hate a total stranger, sight unseen?

Yes, Albanesi found. It absolutely was.

7

Via Monte, Catanzaro

Lending cash at extortionate interest—better known as loan-sharking—is a staple of crime cartels worldwide, and the 'Ndrangheta was no exception. Its other businesses, particularly gambling and street sales of narcotics, commonly leave patrons short of cash to pay their rent and other bills, a problem *'ndranghetisti* are happy to solve. Mob loan sharks had shattered Bolan's family, during another life, and he was always looking for a chance to tap the nearest gangland till, spreading the misery around.

The loan sharks he was looking for tonight operated as Power Finance. Their office was an unobtrusive building with a small sign in front—no need to advertise when word of mouth directed needy borrowers to their facility. And—unlike legitimate S&L firms that kept banker's hours—Power Finance burned the midnight oil, accommodating hungry night dwellers.

Perfect for Bolan's needs.

Loan sharks are big on personal security, and Bolan calculated Power Finance would've doubled up tonight after the recent losses suffered by the Magolino family. He came prepared, with the Beretta ARX-160 slung beneath his lightweight raincoat. Bolan walked through a drizzle from his Fiat to the lighted entryway. Pushing through the unlocked door, he met a stocky male receptionist who looked him over and demanded, "What do you want?"

Try *everything*.

"I need to see your boss," Bolan replied.

The slugger frowned, grunted and asked, "Who are you?"

Bolan showed him the assault rifle and answered, "I'm the guy who'll kill you if you don't get up and take me to the man in charge."

The front man made a point of moving slowly, whether showing some defiance or trying to avoid getting shot— it made no difference as long as he was going in the right direction. Bolan watched the man's hands and kept his distance as the scowling thug led him along a narrow hallway toward a private office in the rear. His escort paused outside the door labeled PRIVATO and raised his eyebrows, as if expecting more instructions.

"Do whatever's normal for you," Bolan said, keeping the gun's muzzle pointed at his chest.

The stocky mobster knocked, no special code, and said, "Hey, boss."

"What?" came from within.

The scowler pushed on through, then broke off to his right, but Bolan tagged him with a 5.56 mm round between the shoulder blades then swung around before he hit the floor to cover two men at the desk. One sat behind it; the other stood off to Bolan's left. He'd been reaching for a hidden sidearm when the ARX-160 found him, freezing him in place.

"I'm making a withdrawal from your bank," Bolan informed the pair of them.

"Say what?" the boss demanded.

Keep it simple, Bolan thought. He answered, "Money. Sack it up."

The top man cut a glance toward his deceased receptionist and asked, "What if I don't."

"It's simple," Bolan said and shot his sidekick through the forehead from a range of ten feet, giving him a crimson halo as he toppled over backward, landing heavily beside the desk.

The boss was nervous now, weighing his options, likely trying to decide if it was better to die now or tell Gianni Magolino he'd handed off a sack of euros to a bandit who'd walked in from the rain.

He chose to live, rolling his desk chair back in the direction of a safe that occupied one corner of his claustrophobic office. Bolan followed, staying safely out of reach in case the loan shark tried to leap at him. When the safe's door opened, he saw stacks of paper money—and a pistol the boss lunged for, snarling like a rabid jackal.

Bolan let him reach it and turn, then shot him in the chest at point-blank range, slamming him over in the rolling chair with arms outflung.

Two minutes in, and Bolan went to work bagging the cash. He appropriated an empty gym bag resting on the safe, stuffing it full of euros that seemed to be banded into bricks of twenty grand apiece. It wouldn't break the 'Ndrangheta's bank, but it would sting Don Magolino.

And for him, the worst was yet to come.

RAF DONDINI GOT the call as he was entering the Paradiso's lobby, with the concierge and desk clerks peering at him, obviously noting that he carried no luggage. He read the caller's number then turned around and walked out of the hotel to take the call outside.

"Where are you?" Aldo Adamo demanded.

"Checking hotels."

"Well, drop that and go to The Flame."

"The casino?"

"Someone hit it," Adamo informed him. "Get over there. Now!"

He was gone before Raf could respond, so Dondini

walked back to the car where the others were waiting and gave them their orders. Gatti groused, as usual, but Pino got them rolling in the right direction. Some ten minutes later, they were parked a half block south of *La Fiamma,* watching firefighters coiling their hoses and trooping in and out.

"Toasted," Gatti said.

Dondini could not disagree, though the nightclub's outer walls looked clean enough, all things considered. Watching the police at work inspired a certain nervousness he could not control, particularly with the heavy weapons barely hidden in their vehicle.

"So, what are we supposed to do?" Pino inquired.

"Adamo didn't say," Dondini answered.

"Typical. He thinks just showing up will solve something," Renni chimed in.

"We need a witness," Dondini suggested. "Somebody who saw the shooters."

"Go ask the cops," Gatti said.

"Shut up. We need someone from the club."

"Call Adamo back," Renni offered.

"You call him," Dondini replied as he got out of the car and angled past the police line and toward a cluster of onlookers, some of them dressed for a night on the town. Scanning faces for any brothers he might recognize, Dondini saw none, but he picked out the club's maître d' in his tux and approached him by shouldering some of the others aside.

"Hey, Carlo. Did you see what happened here?"

The maître d' recognized him as an 'ndranghetisto. He glanced around, made sure no one else was listening and kept his voice pitched low as he replied. "A big man came in with a machine pistol. He forced his way upstairs. I didn't see what happened after that, but there was shooting, then some kind of bomb went off and the alarms were going with the sprinklers."

"Have they said how many men we lost?" Dondini asked.

"Not to me, but they've been taking bodies out in bags. I've counted four so far."

"Describe this man to me."

"Six feet, about two hundred pounds. Well dressed. Dark hair with an olive complexion. He could have been Italian, but his accent wasn't right, you know?"

"Could he have been American?" Dondini pressed.

"Who knows? Maybe, or else British, maybe French."

Dondini removed a photocopy of a driver's license from his pocket and unfolded it. "Is this the man?"

Carlo examined it, frowning. "Could be."

"What do you mean?"

"It looks like him," Carlo replied, "but not exactly right, you know? Something around the eyes is different. Or maybe it's the nose."

"Thanks for nothing."

Carlo shrugged. "What can I say? The Western types all look alike to me. Well, maybe not the Germans."

"If you hear something from the cops, call it in, eh?"

Nodding, Carlo said, "Absolutely."

When he got back to the car, the others asked questions until he silenced them, taking the cell phone from his pocket and speed-dialing Aldo's number. The call was picked up midway through the first ring, as if Aldo had been waiting.

"Yes."

"It was an American," Dondini said, dropping the part about a Brit or Frenchman. They had been called out to hunt for an American. Nothing else made sense.

"The same American?" Adamo asked.

"I showed the picture, but the man who saw him wasn't sure."

"For the love of…" Adamo took a moment, calmed himself, then added, "Who else could it be?"

"That's the same thing I was thinking," Dondini replied.

"Now all you have to do is find him. What's taking so long?"

Guardia di Finanza Headquarters

SIMPLE SOLUTIONS WERE the best sometimes. Rather than roam the streets with Mariana Natale, seeking a safe place to hide her, Captain Basile had brought her back to GDF headquarters. He planned to discuss her future at his office then decide where she should go. If anyone inquired, she was his cousin from Milan, visiting Catanzaro for a holiday.

The only worry was that someone could recognize her... someone on Magolino's payroll. Not impossible, by any means, so he would have to keep her close, bring food and drink into his office from the building's small army of vending machines and let her use the tiny private washroom that a captain's rank provided.

If his efforts failed, Basile knew it could mean both their lives.

When they were settled in his office, Mariana facing him across the desk and fidgeting, Basile said, "I know your family. I understand that helping the authorities must run against the grain for you, but honestly, I see no other way for you to save yourself."

"You can't just...hide me somewhere?"

Basile frowned and shook his head. "You've heard about the country's economic woes, I'm sure. I won't claim to understand it all, but even in the best of times, we never had the funds to simply hide people unless they helped us in some way. It isn't done, my dear."

"So, I must sell my soul."

Basile kept the frown in place. "I'm not a moralist," he answered, "but some people might suggest you've done that very thing already, with Gianni Magolino. Now he's killed your brother in New York and tried to murder you in Catanzaro. It's time for you to choose a path that will decide your future."

"And you hope I'll choose your side."

"Of course," Basile said. "I'm only human, after all, and though it may seem foolish to you, I still cling to certain guidelines of behavior that demand the protection of the innocent from people like your *'ndranghetisti*."

"Not mine," she answered in a small voice. "Not anymore."

"Then it should be a relatively easy choice. You want to live, and I want to put your brother's murderers where they belong. You may be able to assist me. And, if not, an honest effort still should earn a measure of protection for you."

"Ah. 'A measure'?"

He could only shrug and say, "We're both adults. Nothing in life is absolutely guaranteed. You know this from experience."

"I do," she said in almost a whisper. "If I agree, what happens next?"

"I call a magistrate. This lady, I can tell you, I would trust to keep my children safe. It's something of a miracle, I think, that she has not been murdered yet."

"If this is how your reassure informants, it needs work."

"I'll never lie to you," Basile said. "You, of all people, know that with sufficient effort and the proper motivation, anyone can be eliminated. But without the level of protection we can offer you…"

He shrugged and spread his hands, letting silence make his point.

"All right," she said. "I'll do it. But I may not know as much as you suspect. Gianni did not come to me and boast of crimes as he committed them."

"Yet you've lived with him. The family's *padrino*. You have seen him meeting others and overheard him speaking to them, even if it was obscure. Those dates, those conversations, may dovetail with other information from our files to build a case."

"And if they don't?"

"You do your part," Basile said, "and we'll do ours. The bargain does not hinge upon a jury's verdict."

"Very well, Captain. You have a new informant."

"It is the best decision, I assure you." Reaching for the telephone, he said, "I'll make arrangements for you now."

CARLO ALBANESI'S MIND was in a stew of turmoil. He had no doubt the Magolino family would eliminate him if he failed them—or arrange for his dismissal with a leak about the money he'd received in exchange for aiding members of the *cosche*. Prison was not beyond the realm of possibility, and Albanesi knew he wouldn't live a week in custody.

It was a waking nightmare, and the only way he could escape it was to find Mariana Natale. But how?

Albanesi considered praying, but there were limits to his hypocrisy. Why would the God he'd been taught to fear even consider helping him destroy another person to preserve his miserable life? The Lord would probably strike him with a lightning bolt and end his pitiful existence.

Ah, but that was childish fantasy. He'd personally seen the wicked prosper while decent folk suffered. It was enough to cause a loss of faith, assuming he'd had faith to begin with.

Prayer was out, so he'd have to find another way.

Lieutenant Albanesi studied every angle he could think of, scanning files on the computer in his office, looking for a clue—a name—that might direct him to the missing woman. Almost instantly he recognized that he was on the wrong track, listing relatives she would be afraid to visit and the Magolino *cosche* members—once her so-called friends—who would not hesitate to gun her down.

What, then, was left?

He could go home and have a drink and try coming up

with new ideas away from the GDF offices. Albanesi knew he was already pushing it by working at night when he received no pay for overtime and rarely went an inch beyond the bare minimum required by any task. He might invite suspicion if he kept it up, and that was also dangerous.

Leaving his office, Albanese locked the door behind him, turned toward the elevator and froze as he spotted Captain Basile at the far end of the hallway, near an access door that opened to the service stairs.

Basile...and a woman.

She had tawny hair, streaked blond, and a shapely figure. If he had not known better—

Could it be?

He let them pass into the stairwell, neither of them looking back, then hurried after them. Once in the stairs himself, he knew they were descending toward the building's underground garage. The trick now was to keep from losing them without drawing attention to himself. He wasn't sure about the woman yet, would still require at least a quick glimpse of her face, but if his first suspicion was correct, salvation had been laid before him on a silver platter.

Albanesi heard Basile and the woman talking softly as they made their way downstairs. He couldn't understand a word of what they said, nor did he care. As long as he could hear or see them, they were still within his grasp.

Then what?

If the woman was Gianno Magolino's one-time lover, what could Albanesi do about it? Did he have the nerve to kill Basile and abduct her?

No. That would require a great deal more than desperation. Call it raving madness.

He could follow them, however, to find out where they were going and report it to Adamo. That was relatively simple, if he did not make a mess of trailing them.

Two flights below him, Albanesi heard the door to the garage open and close. When it was shut, he hurried down the final steps, no longer creeping for the sake of silence. Speed was critical. He dared not lose Basile and the woman and thereby lose his last chance at redemption.

Or damnation.

Never mind the terminology. He had renewed hope now, and he meant to clutch it like a lifeline thrown out to a drowning man.

Via Francesco Acri, Catanzaro

NEAR MIDNIGHT, BOLAN approached his next target—a trucking company. Guarini Transport, a subsidiary of the Magolino family, had been linked to toxic dumping in Calabria.

Over the past two decades, Italian prosecutors had investigated the suspicious sinking of thirty-odd ships bearing hazardous waste. In roughly half those cases, trucks from Guarini Transport had carried those ill-fated loads to the docks.

But tonight, the firm was going out of business.

Bolan had no difficulty getting past the padlocked gate. He wore a cap pulled low over his eyes, thereby defeating the CCTV cameras he'd spotted on the poles supporting floodlights. The cameras wouldn't catch his face, but they could watch him work and play the action back for Magolino's entertainment.

He went with the Beretta ARX-160 once again—or, more specifically, its 40 mm GLX-160 grenade launcher. The launcher was a single-shot, breech-loaded weapon, not the fastest in the world, but in capable hands such as Bolan's, it did the job.

Ten seconds on the Magolino property, and Bolan had set one rig ablaze, slamming an HE round into the radiator of a heavy hauler. Most of the trucks on hand were semi rigs, but Bolan also counted three articulated dumpers waiting for a load they would never haul. He worked his way around the lot, under the floodlights, blasting each in turn and leaving them to literally burn the midnight oil.

He knew the average list price for a big rig hot off the assembly line. A dozen of them going up in flames slapped Magolino with a punishing loss. Retreating to the open gate when he was finished, Bolan paused to eye his work and reckoned it was adequate.

The only missing feature was credit for the hit.

Driving away, he called Gianni Magolino, got a flunky on the line and didn't bother asking for the boss. "Listen and pay attention," he instructed. "I will not repeat this."

"Go ahead," said the dim bulb on the other end.

"Send someone to Guarini Transport," Bolan said. "You've got a problem."

"What kind of problem?"

"Better see it for yourself," Bolan advised. "And tell your boss that Don Peppino Lanza has a message for him."

"Message?"

"He says, 'Payback is a bitch.'"

He cut the link and drove on as midnight passed into the chill and dark of Wednesday morning. Most of Catanzaro's residents were sleeping now, or on their way to bed, but they'd be waking to hear that hell had come to town.

The good news: it would only last another day, at most.

The bad: for some of them, within that span of time, their world would end.

8

Wednesday—Via Pastaioli, Catanzaro

Between GDF headquarters and the safe house, Albanesi
had nearly lost Captain Basile and the woman twice. He
had managed to catch them both times, though, hanging
back just enough to be hidden in late-night traffic while
still maintaining visual contact. Now that they'd reached
their final destination, he was parked a block downrange
and peering through a pair of opera glasses he kept in his
car's glove compartment. They were not the best for high-
tech surveillance, but they would suffice.

He saw Basile stop his car outside a modest house and
walk around to open the woman's door. Then Basile led
her to the entryway, where two men dressed in inexpensive
suits stood waiting to receive them. All four went inside.
Lieutenant Albanesi waited, trembling from nervous en-
ergy. He could have benefited from a drink—grappa, perhaps—but he had no alcohol on board tonight.

Making a mental note to remedy that situation, Albanesi watched the house while shooting frequent glances
at his side and rearview mirrors, anxious about someone
sneaking up on him while he was distracted. He considered calling Adamo as soon as the woman was inside the
house, but he'd worried she might come out again and drive
off with Basile.

Worse, he worried that Adamo would command him to rush in—one man against the three of them—and snatch the woman for delivery to Magolino. If that happened, Albanesi knew he'd make a mess of it. What if he couldn't pull the trigger? What if he was terrified and soiled himself?

No. He had reached the limit of his capability and recognized that fact. He was a sneak, a spy, but not a soldier. Not much of a police officer, either, if he thought about it honestly, but he maintained a more or less professional façade. One had to draw the line somewhere, and although he thought he could kill if threatened—or if he were paid enough, with little risk of being caught—it was too much for him to crash a safe house on his own, like some kind of commando in a movie.

Half an hour passed, perhaps a little more, before Basile left the house alone and drove away. That told Albanesi all he had to know, and he'd palmed his phone before the captain's taillights faded out of sight.

"Hello."

He recognized the voice, Adamo's main houseman. "It's me," Albanesi said. "Tell him I've found her."

"Hold the line"

Thirty seconds later, Adamo answered. "Where is she?"

Albanesi rattled off the address, waited for Adamo to repeat it, then said, "Right."

"Stay and keep an eye on them," Adamo ordered. "Call back if they try to move her before my people get there."

Albanesi did not want to linger, but he had no choice. "As you wish, sir."

The line went dead, Adamo satisfied that he would wait and watch like a faithful dog hoping for a reward. It galled him, but he'd made his choice the first time he accepted money from the 'Ndrangheta. Nothing serious the first time, just some paperwork misplaced, but after that, there had been no refusing them.

What if the guards *did* leave with Mariana? He would

call, of course, and be ordered to pursue them, helping the appointed killers track their prey. It troubled Albanesi, knowing his actions would condemn two officers he'd never met before, but what choice did he have? It was too late for him to grow a backbone. Defiance would inevitably lead to death—or worse, exposure, with the loss of his career, his reputation, everything. And after he had been humiliated, he'd likely be sent to prison, and he could still be murdered any time Adamo or his master chose to give the order.

Albanesi drew his pistol, taking comfort from its firm weight in his hand. He checked the mirrors once more, then settled in to watch the silent house, hoping the targets would not budge before Adamo's soldiers came to root them out.

And if he made it out and went home to sleep, Lieutenant Albanesi prayed he would not dream.

Via Veraldi, Catanzaro

BOLAN'S NEXT STOP was a clothing warehouse. Not his normal kind of target, but this warehouse was stuffed to the rafters with counterfeit designer duds—Dior, Fendi, Gucci, Versace, Prada, Dolce & Gabbana, take your pick. Cheap knockoffs tagged with fake designer labels swamped the markets in America and Europe, ripping off the public and designers alike. Fashion meant less than nothing to the Executioner, but when it helped to keep a crime cartel afloat, he took an interest.

Like now.

The warehouse was a nondescript facility. Its name—Trapani Products—gave no hint of what might lie within or who the owners were, but it had turned up on his list of 'Ndrangheta properties in Catanzaro. The bogus merchandise represented several million euros for the Magolino family.

About to be an ashen memory.

He went in through the back door, used the tire iron from his Fiat Panda on the padlock, then slipped the tool through his belt. His 40 mm launcher was loaded with an XM1060 thermobaric round, the ultimate incendiary, known in common parlance as a fuel-air bomb. The warehouse would be nothing but a giant tinder box.

For Bolan's purposes, he didn't have to trespass far inside the building. All he needed was a clean shot toward the rear, beyond the countless cartons filled with fabric. No guards had surfaced to confront him, but if any were concealed inside the warehouse, maybe sleeping on the job, they had a rude awakening in store for them.

Bolan aimed his launcher toward the far wall of the warehouse, approximately a hundred feet away. Precision wasn't necessary; hell, he didn't really have to aim at all— just point and let it fly. The launcher made a muffled *pop,* and the projectile struck down range, exploding on impact, a rising, roiling ball of flame advancing swiftly toward the spot where Bolan stood.

He didn't hang around to greet it, exiting the place as rapidly as possible, feeling the heat on his back and scalp. A few more seconds wasted, and he would have been consumed along with Magolino's knockoff garments.

Out in the fresh night air, the back door slammed behind him, Bolan jogged to his waiting car and stowed the ARX-160 in the space behind the driver's seat. He risked another moment at the curb, the Panda's engine humming softly, while he watched the warehouse start to glow from the inside until it had the aspect of a giant lantern. When the first flames finally erupted through a row of skylights, Bolan put the Fiat in gear and rolled out.

Despite the time he'd spent with Mariana, getting her squared away, his blitz was more or less on schedule. Running slightly later than anticipated, he was still on track to have the campaign finished in a day, at most. Then he could turn his thoughts to getting out of Italy and back Stateside.

As usual, Bolan traveled with a backup passport and supporting documents, although he had not seen a need to use them yet. He'd save them for the day he booked a new flight from Calabria to Rome, probably switching airports to avoid Lamezia Terme.

Which still, of course, assumed he'd survive the Catanzaro mission.

That was never guaranteed, but Bolan liked to take the positive approach whenever possible. In this case, he was positive that Wednesday would be worse than Tuesday for the Magolino family.

He would bet his life on that.

THE CALL HAD come at half past midnight, drawing Raf Dondini and his soldiers from their aimless scouring of city streets to a specific house on Via Pastaioli. When they got there, Dondini saw a pair of headlights flash ahead of them, and he had Arturo Pino pass the target dwelling, creeping forward till his open window was directly opposite the driver's window of a Fiat Bravo parked against the curb.

He did not recognize the nervous-looking man behind the Bravo's wheel, but he knew a cop when he smelled one. "What's the story?" he inquired before the cop could speak.

"You took a damn long time to get here," the fat policeman said.

"Just be glad we're here at all," Dondini replied. "Is she inside the house?"

The porky face bobbed once in affirmation. "With at least two men."

"Who are they?"

A shrug this time. "They could be GDF. Maybe Carabinieri."

"When you say, 'at least two men…'"

"I saw two. There may still be more inside."

"All right, we'll handle it. Get out of here."

Dismissing the fat stranger, he told Pino, "Drive around the block and park short of the house."

Pino did as he was told without any dramatic screech of tires or racing of the engine that was likely to alarm their targets in the safe house. That was almost laughable, Dondini thought, believing anyplace in Catanzaro could be safe from members of the Magolino family.

That was a grave mistake. Fatal, in fact.

Adamo's orders were specific: kill whoever had been left to guard the woman and retrieve her—alive and fit for rigorous interrogation. Failing that, Adamo wanted cell phone photos proving she was dead, once and for all. Dondini liked the second option best, but he would try to give Adamo what he wanted.

One live whore trussed up for the slaughter.

As they parked, his soldiers checked their weapons one last time, then crawled out of the vehicle and stretched their legs, standing together in the dark between two widely separated streetlights.

"Nothing fancy," Dondini advised them. "We go in and do the job. The woman lives, if possible. No hasty 'accidents,' unless you want to deal with Aldo personally. Renni and Gatti, slip around in back. You've got two minutes, then I'm going through the front door with Pino. Everyone, be sure of who you're killing when you pull the trigger, eh?"

They nodded at him, silent, all of them on edge, then Renni and Gatti moved off into darkness, circling quietly around behind the target house. Dondini checked his watch and started counting down the time until they made their move. One minute in, he led Pino down the sidewalk, then turned right and crept on to the only porch he'd seen with no light burning.

It was strange, he thought, how people trying *not* to draw attention so often did one thing that had the opposite effect.

At the two-minute mark, Dondini raised his Styer AUG

and fired a muffled three-round burst into the door's dead-bolt, then kicked it in and charged through, Pino on his heels with the Franchi SPAS-15.

They caught two men rushing to intercept them, one emerging from the kitchen and the other from a sort of parlor to their left, where he'd been watching *Naked News* on TV. Dondini shot him in the chest and left the chef to Pino.

By then, Renni and Gatti were through the back door and had started scouring the other rooms. Dondini moved to join them, but they found the girl almost immediately. The two men grinned as they dragged her from a bedroom out into the hallway.

She was trembling and tearful, but she marked Dondini as the leader and returned his stare without flinching, seemingly prepared to die. "Get on with it," she spat at him.

"Relax," he told her, putting on a smile. "We're going for a little ride."

CAPTAIN BASILE STOOD outside the house and watched the second body bag emerging on its gurney, navigated by a pair of ambulance attendants whose vitality and good looks painfully reminded him that he was middle-aged. No, scratch that. Middle age meant halfway through a normal life span, and at fifty-four, Basile had to grant that he was well past it.

Two dead, both honest men with families, and no trace remained of Mariana Natale. Basile wondered why the damned *'ndranghetisti* had not simply killed her on the spot, but that thought led him onto darker paths that turned his stomach, so he focused on the better question.

How had they discovered where she was?

Basile had taken every precaution to keep Mariana secure, bypassing his superiors, arranging for a pair of officers he trusted to watch over her, assigning them that duty with last-minute calls that brought them from home. The homes he would be forced to visit now, breaking the grim news to their wives and children, facing their grief and rage.

Two men, besides himself, had known where Mariana was, and both of them were dead now. Had one of his two trusted friends betrayed Basile, dooming himself in the process? It was possible, of course, but so unlikely Basile put the prospect out of mind.

How else could Mariana have been traced?

His telephone at headquarters was more or less secure. Basile swept it periodically for taps and checked his office for illicit microphones, but so many devices were on the high-tech market nowadays, he couldn't keep up with them all.

Another possibility: he'd been seen with Mariana at headquarters, either coming in or going out, and followed to the safe house. That seemed most likely, but Basile thought he'd been careful on the drive to Via Pastaioli. Was it possible he'd been distracted by the woman or by thoughts of her American rescuer and the battle plans he'd laid for Catanzaro?

Maybe.

Probably.

Basile cursed himself and dug fingernails into his palms but found no sanctuary in the trifling pain. Perhaps a drink would help. Leave the forensics team to sweep the house, and come back in a half hour or so to receive their report.

Basile turned from the house and almost collided with Carlo Albanesi, waddling up the walkway from the street.

"I heard the call about officers down," Albanesi said. "It there something I can do to help?"

"Nothing that comes to mind, Lieutenant. Were you still at headquarters?"

"Just leaving to go home. Who have we lost?"

"Two men from GICO," Basile answered, referring to the GDF's organized crime investigators. "I doubt you knew them."

"A loss all the same. Our brothers, eh, Captain?"

Brothers. Basile nodded silently and told his overweight subordinate, "You may as well go home."

"Well, if you're sure…"

"Go on. You'll hear enough about this later, at the office."

"All right then. Good night, Captain."

"Good morning, Lieutenant."

At least Basile would be rid of Albanesi for a while. He still wanted that drink, or several, but he'd reconsidered. It was best to keep his mind clear as he tried to work out who had managed to betray him, killing two good men while they were at it.

When he had the answer to that question, then Basile would be faced with a decision. In the meantime, though, he needed help.

Who could he trust in Catanzaro now?

Someone who had not been corrupted by the 'Ndrangheta, by the Mafia or by any other source of vile contagion. Someone new and unfamiliar to the enemy.

He thought of Scott Parker, realizing instantly that he had no means of contacting the American. Or did he?

Glancing at his watch, Basile subtracted six hours to get the current time for Washington, D.C. If he could reach the man who'd called him earlier that evening asking for a favor, he might get one in return. Basile would not know until he tried.

Retreating from the murder house to stand beneath a nearby streetlight, Basile found the number in his call log, hit REDIAL, and waited for someone to answer at the other end, nearly five thousand miles away.

Via Alessandro Turco, Catanzaro

BOLAN WAS TWO blocks from his next target when the sat phone hummed at him, a breach of protocol so startling that he snatched it up before it had a chance to sound again. He didn't recognize the number on the LED screen and frowned as he answered cautiously.

"Hello?"

"I hope you will accept my most sincere apology," the caller said.

"Captain Basile."

"Yes. The very same."

"How did you get this number?"

"From a friend we have in common, I believe," the captain said. "In Washington?"

Bolan pulled over to the curb and left the Fiat Panda's engine running. Trying to imagine how the captain could have got his number without asking Hal, he came up blank. Because the sat phone had no GPS device installed, he felt secure in chatting with Basile at the roadside, but he meant to keep it brief, regardless.

"What can I do for you?" Bolan asked.

"I'm afraid I have bad news," Basile said. "I must apologize once more for being negligent."

"You want to spell that out for me?"

"With Mariana. She has been abducted."

"How?" Basile couldn't miss the cutting edge of steel in Bolan's voice.

"We still don't know. I took precautions and chose my closest and most trusted friends to guard her. They are both dead now, and she is…gone."

Bolan swallowed his first response. Cursing the captain would accomplish nothing. Thinking rapidly, he asked, "How long?"

"The shooting was reported to us—" A pause, likely Basile looking at his watch "—one hour and three minutes ago."

A lifetime. Mariana could be dead by now or hurt so badly that she was praying for death. The good news, if it *was* good news: the hit team had not killed her on the spot. Which meant someone higher up the 'Ndrangheta food chain wanted her alive, if only for interrogation or a savage payback.

So, there *might* be time. And he was wasting it.

"Here's what you do," he told Basile. "Go back over every move you made between the garden and your safe house. Make a list of anyone who might have seen the two of you together, even if it seems improbable."

"I could—"

"Just make the list," Bolan said. "Handle the cops yourself. Interrogate them any way you can. As for civilians, call me back with names and tell me where to find them."

Basile didn't question that but asked him, "What will you be doing in the meantime?"

"Burning down Gianni Magolino's world," Bolan replied before he cut the link.

He wasted no time second-guessing himself. He and Mariana had discussed her options, and she'd voted for protective custody. Unfortunately, Bolan couldn't let it go at that. He'd rescued Mariana once, so simply dismissing her to any fate that Magolino had in mind was not an option he could live with.

The bottom line: retrieving Mariana now, alive, might be impossible. But punishing her captors was a game Bolan had played before. In fact, he was a master of reprisals, as the Magolino family was just about to learn.

It even fit into his program, more or less. His goal had been disruption of the 'Ndrangheta and elimination of its Catanzaro leadership. Full speed ahead on that score, but he had to put a new twist on the game.

Bolan could not kill Magolino or his second in command until he'd sent a message and they'd had an opportunity to answer him. He would negotiate for Mariana's freedom, see if Magolino played along and still feel free to double-cross the mobster when it suited him. For all the rhetoric about the 'Ndrangheta's honor, Bolan found that integrity was nonexistent in the underworld. And because he played by their rules, for the most part, lying to a gangster did not trouble him at all.

The gangsters also would be lying when they dealt with him.

But they would have incentive to deliver Mariana, even if she only served as bait.

Bolan pulled into traffic, on his way to blitz Gianni Magolino's world.

9

Viale Alvaro Corrado, Catanzaro

"You have done well, Aldo. I am pleased," Gianni Magolino said.

Adamo let himself relax a little, still not smiling openly but starting to believe he had redeemed himself. It was a stroke of luck that had probably saved his life.

As if reading his thoughts, Aldo's *padrino* asked, "How did you manage it?"

A lie at this point would be perilous, but he could always shade the truth. "One of our people at the GDF saw Mariana with a captain. On my orders, the cop followed them. From that point, it was simple."

"Two dead policemen," Magolino said, then shrugged. "It is a small price for our family's security. I won't forget this, Aldo."

"It's nothing."

Magolino smiled. "You are too modest."

"Well…"

"Your men must be rewarded for their service also."

"As you say, *padrino.* I shall see to it."

"But not too highly, eh? We don't want to inflate their egos."

"No, sir," Adamo replied, smiling at the little joke.

"I must see Mariana now," Magolino said. "We have so much to discuss."

"Of course, *padri*—"

The house man, Gino Zucco, barged into Magolino's office. "Excuse me, *padrino,*" he said, extending a cordless phone to Magolino.

"Who is it?" the boss demanded.

"He won't say, but he knows about the woman and our dead brothers."

"Does he?" Magolino took the phone, handling it gingerly, as if it might explode. Putting on a stoic face, he spoke into the instrument. "Who's this?"

Adamo could not hear the caller's reply, but he saw Magolino stiffen slightly, knuckles blanching as his grip on the telephone tightened. His side of the conversation grew stilted. "Yes…I see…What makes you think…You are assuming…No…I can't agree to that, since…Very well, then. Do your worst."

Those last words spoken, Magolino switched the phone off, placed it back in Gino's hand and turned his full attention to Adamo.

"The American," he declared, putting a twist in Aldo's gut.

"Parker?"

"If we believe him," Magolino said.

Aldo asked the first question that came to mind. "How did he get your number?"

Magolino shrugged. "That's beside the point. He says Mariana must be freed at once."

"Or what?" Adamo asked.

"He says the losses we have suffered since this afternoon are merely—how did he describe it? Ah, yes—'a preview of coming attractions.' He threatens to wipe out our *cosche* and kill both of us in the bargain."

Adamo felt a sudden chill. "He mentioned us specifically?"

"Your name was mentioned, Aldo. Does it frighten you?"

"Certainly not!"

"Good. You've done so well with Mariana that I have a new job for you. Find this Scott Parker. As with Mariana, I prefer that you capture him alive. But failing that, bring me his head. I'll give it to Giacomo D'Ascanio."

Adamo swallowed the revulsion he felt each time the taxidermist's name came up. D'Ascanio worked on selected trophies for the personal collection Magolino kept in a secret location. To Aldo's certain knowledge, it included eight preserved and mounted specimens that Magolino visited from time to time, as he said, to relax.

Adamo nearly answered that his soldiers had been seeking Scott Parker since the killings at Le Croci, having no success, but he was wise enough to bite his tongue. Instead of pleading failure, when he'd only just regained Magolino's confidence, he said, "I will find him, *padrino*. You can count on it."

"Before he ruins us, I hope," Magolino said. "Before he kills us all."

Nearly choking on his words, Adamo replied, "Trust me, *padrino*."

But where would he begin?

Leaving his master's office, Aldo wondered if he'd condemned himself. Would his head be the next one found in Magolino's trophy case?

Via Alessandro Turco, Catanzaro

AFTER HIS ROADSIDE conversation with Captain Basile, Bolan rolled on toward his next target. It was a brothel catering to wealthy men and women—no discrimination on the 'Ndrangheta's part, where money was concerned—disguised, more or less, as a stately private home. The girls worked mostly by appointment, although a drop-in john with ample cash to spend could always be accommodated. If any neighbors kept track of the traffic flowing in and out, night after night, they were wise enough to keep their heads down and not bother the city's overworked police.

Mack Bolan, on the other hand, was making time to put the operation out of business.

One trick of a sniper's trade is patience, the ability to wait for hours—sometimes days—until the perfect shot presents itself. Tonight, however, he was on the clock. Bolan could hear it ticking in his head, time running out for Mariana while he prowled the streets, selecting targets from the list he'd drawn up in advance. The blitz technique demanded rapid-fire attacks, incessant violence, a message driven home that every moment of delay would cost his enemies more men, more property, more money until Bolan had been satisfied.

It was a method that had worked for him in past campaigns, but in some cases the blitz had failed to rescue hostages. Sometimes he got the word too late; other times, Bolan's enemies were tough enough and crazy enough to risk retaliation, thereby escalating violence against themselves. He didn't have a feel yet for Gianni Magolino, but it made good sense to play the odds and see what happened next.

So, on he drove, around the looping course of Via Alessandro Turco and toward his target, which stood on two well-tended acres, grass and sturdy shade trees all around it. Bolan parked in front, mounted the concrete steps and rang the bell, making no effort to conceal the submachine gun carried at his side.

The door opened almost immediately to reveal a smiling woman in her thirties, dressed as if she were preparing for a night on the town. Except the night was nearly over, and a glimpse of Bolan's weapon wiped the trained smile from her face.

"Don't shoot!" she implored.

"Don't make me."

"I won't," she said.

"First thing," he told her, when they were inside, "Where's the fire alarm?"

"But...there's no fire."

"Not yet," he said and drew his jacket back just far enough to show her a grenade clipped on his belt.

She led him through the foyer and around a corner, to a parlor where a fire alarm's pull-handle was discreetly hidden by a hanging tapestry. Bolan grasped the metal lever and pulled down. A raucous clamoring began reverberating through the house.

The result was almost instantaneous. From every doorway on the second floor, a clamoring stampede of nude or half-dressed men and women rushed to find the nearest exit, barely taking time to glance at Bolan or the whorehouse madam as they passed.

"You've made a serious mistake," the hostess warned him.

Bolan didn't answer. He was waiting for the guards, and in another moment, there they were. Three men, dressed casually—blazers over slacks and open-collared shirts—all armed and focused on the stranger in their midst. They should have opened fire on him immediately, but their point man hesitated when he saw the brothel's manager at Bolan's side, and that was all the edge Bolan required.

His first short, nearly silent burst gutted the leader of the pack and sent him tumbling through an awkward roll, leaving a bloody trail on the white shag carpeting. The two remaining men both aimed pistols at Bolan, but their chance had come and gone. He strafed them from the ground, spattering the second-story wall with blood and bits of tissue as the dying shooters fell together, tangled up in a macabre embrace.

"Are there more?" Bolan asked the madam.

"No." Trembling, she shook her head emphatically. "No more. They are the only ones."

She waited, seeming to expect a bullet of her own, but Bolan nodded toward the nearest door and said, "Get out of here. Tell Magolino this keeps up until he sets the woman free. Got that?"

"I understand," she assured him, breaking for the exit and the night beyond it.

Bolan found the kitchen, turned the range on high and ripped its gas line from the wall. Retreating to the doorway, he unclipped a frag grenade and lobbed it toward the hissing stove, then made a swift retreat.

Hellfire. And he had only just begun.

Guardia di Finanza Headquarters

CAPTAIN BASILE KNEW he'd made a devil's bargain, but he saw no viable alternative. Mariana Natale had been left in his care, and now she was lost, and two of his most trusted officers had paid with their lives for his negligence. He could not think of any explanation for the safe house raid, and if she died, too—a likely prospect, in Basile's view—he knew it would trouble him for the remainder of his days.

There was nothing he could do about it on his own, so he had picked the only option that remained. It would mean more killing, more destruction in the city Basile was sworn to serve and protect, but what else could he do?

If there was any chance at all for Mariana, he was bound to try it.

And if Scott Parker failed to rescue her a second time… what then?

The list, for one thing. He had vowed to list the names of anyone who might have seen him with the woman, but the top page of the notepad on his desk remained a mocking blank. Basile had been cautious when escorting Mariana to his office—or, at least, he believed he had been. Walking from Villa Margherita back to GDF headquarters, they had met no one along the way. Not in the park or on the street, not in the parking lot or hallways leading to his office. She had not emerged until they left, together, for the drive out to the safe house.

Who had seen her with him? When and how had it occurred without his notice?

Was he truly that oblivious to his surroundings, even when the stakes were life and death?

A rapping on the office door distracted him. Basile glanced up from the damned note pad and said, "Come in."

Carlo Albanesi entered. "Excuse me, Captain. I was passing by and I saw your light. You're working late this evening."

"As are you, Lieutenant."

"It's the killings," Albanesi said. "They're calling everyone from home."

Basile nodded. That was standard when an officer was killed on duty. All hands turned out to participate in the investigation, find the murderers and bring them in, dead or alive. Of course, it rarely worked that way if *mafiosi* or *'ndranghetisti* were involved. With them, unless the crime was witnessed by police or one of the participants confessed, the case was likely to remain unsolved. And even if their names were known, beyond a doubt, achieving justice was an iffy proposition.

"I won't keep you then," Basile said. "You must have work to do."

The lieutenant bobbed his head, then said, "I thought there might be something I could do for you."

"Such as?"

That brought a wobbly shrug. "I'm sorry, Captain, but I didn't think that far ahead."

"There is a question I might ask you," Basile said.

"Ah. What is it?"

"When I was in the station earlier tonight, nine-thirty, maybe ten o'clock, did you see me, by any chance?"

"See you?" A hint of color rose in Albanesi's flabby cheeks. "No, I'm afraid not. Should I have?"

The bastard was lying, and it chilled Basile to his core. It should have come as no surprise, with Albanesi's reputation, but for some reason, Basile had not thought he would be party to the murder of two fellow officers.

Smiling as if his heart had not begun to hammer in his chest, Basile said, "No reason. I just thought…"

"What?" Albanesi prodded him.

"It's nothing, really. Earlier, I had a visitor and meant to introduce you."

Albanesi's little rat eyes shifted nervously around the office, as if looking for a place to hide. "Who was this visitor?" he asked.

"It's not important," Basile said. "Anyway, the chance is lost."

"Pity. Well, I'll leave you to your work and return to mine."

"Good night, Lieutenant."

"Good morning, Captain."

Albanesi closed the door behind him as he left, Basile's eyes still boring into it.

He knew the traitor now, beyond a doubt. But what was he going to do about it?

Feeling twice his age, Basile pushed the notebook to one side, removed his pistol from its holster and began the ritual of field stripping to clean and oil its working parts.

It never hurt, he thought, to be prepared.

Via Nuova, Catanzaro

BOLAN WAS BACK at the beginning, where he'd first seen Mariana in the hands of men who meant to kill her. No one was in the office building now; even the nightly cleaning crew had done their work and left for home. The place was locked, no watchman in attendance for security.

It was a bonfire waiting to be lit.

He parked in back this time, invisible to drivers passing by on Via Nuova. A cool breeze welcomed Bolan as he stepped out of the Fiat Panda, then leaned back inside for just a moment to retrieve the ARX-160 from its place behind the driver's seat.

He could have phoned Gianni Magolino to see if he'd changed his mind about releasing Mariana, but it wouldn't hurt to make another fiery sacrifice or two before he made that call. The more pain Magolino felt before they spoke again, the better it would be for Bolan's cause.

Or, if the mobster dug his heels in and refused to budge, at least it was a preview of the carnage set to come his way.

Knowing Mariana might be dead did not change Bolan's basic plan. Until he had some concrete proof that she was gone, forever beyond help, he would proceed as he had promised, burning down the mobsters' world.

And if she *was* dead, it would change nothing but the pace and raw ferocity of his assault. In that case, Magolino might—or might not—live to see his empire crumble at his feet, a heap of reeking ashes. Whether he survived to rue the loss or not, that was the Executioner's end game, and he would see it through.

He primed the GLX-160 launcher with another thermobaric round and sighted on a second-story window, heedless of whoever might be renting out the office space. Gianni Magolino owned the building, and its loss would be another blow to his finances. Next, Bolan considered, he might hit the 'Ndrangheta's favorite construction company, well known for cutting corners and inflating costs. A little something else to rob the godfather of sleep on what might be his final night on Earth.

The thermo round punched through its target window pane and detonated well inside the room beyond, a flare of light that blossomed in a heartbeat, spreading out and sucking at the window's blinds as it drew air in from the night. It made a hungry snarling sound, reminding Bolan of a giant garbage disposal at work, then two adjacent windows shattered, raining glass into the parking lot.

He could have walked around the building, lobbed another round in through a different window, maybe on another floor, but he was done here. By the time the Catanzaro fire brigade arrived, the office block would be a flaming wreck, fit only for a wrecking ball. One more prime property scratched off the list of Magolino family holdings, and he had a fair list yet to go.

Bolan replaced his weapon in its nook behind the driver's seat and rolled out of there. If any witnesses observed his car leaving while the fire spread, they might easily mistake his stolen ride for a police car, adding more confusion to the mix.

Next up, a sporting goods emporium whose owner funneled weapons and explosives to the 'Ndrangheta, giving Magolino's family an edge over its local enemies. The man in charge was not a sworn *'ndranghetisti,* but he served the family for profit, and the hardware he supplied had terminated countless lives over the years. Putting him out of business would be Bolan's gift to Catanzaro and to law enforcement, one more job for which he would receive no thanks.

But it would satisfy him all the same.

And if Gianni Magolino still had any doubts about releasing Mariana, if he balked the next time Bolan called, the godfather would discover quickly that the worst was still to come.

Viale Alvaro Corrado, Catanzaro

"YOU SEE NOW, Mariana, that you can't escape me."

Sitting with her wrists bound to the curved arms of a wooden chair, ankles secured by duct tape to its legs, she stared at Magolino with a grim, hopeless expression.

"Nothing to say?" he goaded. "No show today? No effort to excuse yourself?"

"Would it do any good?" she asked him sullenly.

"I doubt it very much. But if you care to try…"

"You sentenced me to death for nothing, and I ran away to save myself. You have been fleeing retribution all your life, Gianni."

"There's my girl," he gloated. "I was worried your spirit might be broken, and we haven't even started yet. Later, perhaps."

"Then do your worst, and go to hell. You'll die for this," she told him.

"That's what your friend said, more or less."

"My friend?"

"The American. Parker, I believe he calls himself."

"You spoke to him?"

"He called to threaten me. An ant insults a lion. Should I worry, Mariana?"

Peering at him, she replied, "You are already worried. I can smell it on you."

He was moving forward, drawing back one arm to strike, when Gino Zucco barged into the room, holding the cordless telephone in front of him. "Forgive me, *padrino*," he said. "It's *him* again."

Magolino grimaced as he dropped his arm and unclenched his fist to accept the phone. He raised it to his ear and turned his back on Mariana so she could not see his face as he addressed the caller.

"Yes?"

"The price keeps going up," said the familiar voice. "How much is Mariana worth to you?"

"More than you can imagine," Magolino said. "I don't negotiate with terrorists."

The laugh surprised him. "That's rich," Bolan said, "considering the source. How much are you out so far? Six million? More?"

"Honor counts for more than money," Magolino answered.

This time, Parker's laughter stung him like a slap across the face. "Your call," said the American. "Next time, maybe I'll have a word with your successor."

And the line went dead. Again.

He swiveled back toward Mariana, glowering. "You look a little pale, Gianni," she observed.

"Do I?" Magolino felt the rage boil up inside him. "*Do I?*" Charging forward, with the phone still in his hand, he drove his fist into her face. The wooden chair flew over backward, taking Mariana with it. Blood flowed freely from her nostrils as she lay before him, whimpering.

"Perhaps what you need is a new perspective." Turning back to Gino Zucco, he said, "Gather up the soldiers. We are leaving for Tropea. Fifteen minutes!"

"Yes, *padrino!*"

Zucco vanished, scuttling to obey his order. Magolino walked a circle around Mariana, who was lying like a capsized turtle, helpless at his feet. He thought of all she would suffer when they reached his rural hideaway, and he had to smile.

"I have a colleague you've never met," he said. "The doctor. He tends my soldiers when they're injured and cannot afford the scrutiny of hospitals, but he has other talents, too. Keeping traitors alive during interrogation is his specialty."

The fear, perhaps combined with pain, made Mariana roll her head away from him, retching.

"Now, look," he said. "You've soiled the carpet. What a sad, pathetic creature you've become." Kneeling beside her, bending closer, Magolino dropped his voice until it was a whisper. "But you haven't reached the bottom yet, my beauty. The worst is definitely still ahead for you."

10

Via Scuola Agraria, Catanzaro

The *Società Calabrese Sociale* was, at least ostensibly, a sporting club open to any man of Calabrian birth. In fact, it was an 'Ndrangheta hangout where made members of the Magolino family killed time and partied between assignments. Bolan did not expect a large crowd to be present in the predawn hours of this hectic Wednesday morning, but the club was on his route to one of Magolino's high-class restaurants, and he was stopping by to put it out of business.

Perched on a rooftop opposite the club, across two lanes of sparse traffic, he used the ARX-160's thermal sight to zero in on the club's air-conditioning unit—or, more specifically, an air-intake vent the size of a street-corner mailbox slot. The Qioptiq VIPIR-2 put him up close and personal as Bolan stroked the launcher's trigger, sending a thermobaric round toward impact.

It made a clean drop through the aperture, into the a/c system's guts, and detonated far enough inside to send flames gushing out of vents along the whole top floor, lighting the walls, the acoustic ceiling tiles and the carpets on fire. He couldn't hear the fire alarms begin to clamor and wondered if their circuits had been fried, but when the upstairs windows shattered, there was no mistaking the black smoke escaping through their empty frames to foul the night.

Bolan waited, trusting the club to burn with no more help from him, pausing to see if any Magolino soldiers tried to flee the spreading conflagration. Sixty seconds later, the front doors opened and a pair of sleepy-looking mobsters lurched onto the sidewalk, followed shortly by three more. They milled about, gesticulating as they jabbered back and forth, while Bolan watched them through the sight.

Enough.

Bolan shot the soldier farthest to his left, punching a 5.56 mm tumbler through his lungs from eighty yards. Before the first one dropped, he had his next mark lined up through the VIPIR-2, a clean shot through the forehead just above his right eye, taking out the whole rear quadrant of his skull.

That set the others scrambling, one breaking to Bolan's left, two to his right. He tracked the lonely runner, overtaking him before he reached a nearby alley's mouth, and drilled him with a shot between the shoulder blades.

That left two, both clawing pistols out from underneath their loose shirttails as they kept running. Bolan swung around to follow them, scoping the leader first and putting a hot round through his armpit as he ran. The mobster dropped and rolled, tripping his young friend midstride. The last survivor of the five fell heavily, losing his pistol in the process, then sprang up and scrambled after it, determined not to face his death unarmed.

It didn't help.

The fifth round out of Bolan's rifle burned a tunnel through the panting mobster's slack-jawed face and slapped his head back like a solid uppercut. A scarlet spume erupted from the dying target's mouth as he fell over backward, sprawling on the sidewalk like a rag doll.

Finished.

Bolan retraced his path across the office building's

broad, flat roof, then down the fire escape. Two minutes later he was in the Fiat Panda and away from the scene before the first distant whooping of sirens was audible.

Progress? Not yet. But Bolan had to think he was getting closer.

Every businessman, legitimate or otherwise, kept one eye on the bottom line. Gianni Magolino knew he was bleeding cash. The only question now was how much he would sacrifice while trying to save face.

Guardia di Finanza Headquarters

CAPTAIN BASILE LISTENED to the radio behind his desk, as one report after another charted carnage in his city. He was tired of going out on calls, no longer cared to stand before a burned-out edifice with corpses lined up on the sidewalk, waiting for their last ride to the morgue. He'd seen enough and was oppressed by a conviction that the bloodshed was, at least in part, his fault.

He had not summoned the American to Catanzaro, it was true, but they had made a bargain, and Basile hadn't kept his side of it. And failing that, he had reached out to Scott Parker, set him loose upon the Magolino family, in full knowledge of what his call for help would mean.

Arson and murder. Slaughter in the streets.

But now, some of the crackling bulletins told another story. There had been three reports, so far, of raids staged by a group of several gunmen, who'd strafed Magolino properties and in one case lobbed hand grenades. Basile knew Parker was alone in Catanzaro—or believed he was, at any rate. Who were the other gunmen prowling through the early morning darkness, striking with precision and vanishing as swiftly as they came?

Basile was accustomed to the violence that sputtered between criminal cartels. *'Ndranghetisti* fought with *mafiosi,* and at times, both skirmished with intruding *camor-*

risti. In their cutthroat world, there were no courts to settle
family disputes, no arbitration board to rule on squabbles
over territory. Jungle law applied to every situation, save for
rare occurrences when one group condescended to perform
some service for another at a price. War was the norm, and
although it generally claimed its victims singly and more
or less discreetly, public outbreaks weren't unknown, by
any means.

A gang war? At the very time the American stalked
Gianni Magolino's men?

What were the odds?

Basile had informants, but no one was presently available for comment. He'd spent the past half hour reaching
out to them, but all his calls went straight to voice mail and
he left no messages, fearful of leaving someone fatally exposed. Frustrated, he'd flirted with the thought of ringing
up Lieutenant Albanesi and asking for a private meeting
well away from headquarters. The urge was strong, but
in his heart, Basile was not sure he could trust himself to
keep from pounding Albanesi's fat face.

It was not the time for that. Not yet.

But if the grim American could not recover Mariana—if
she was already dead or had been caught up in the expand-
ing violence—Basile thought he might require a taste of
retribution before he could sleep at night. He had no way
to prove his suspicion, no real hope of prosecuting Albanesi under law, but could Basile face himself again if he
did nothing?

He was still at least ten years away from full retirement
with a pension he could live on, more or less. A false step
now, much less a criminal offense, could mean the end of
his career, his reputation, everything. But when he thought
about the satisfaction it might give him, he couldn't help
smiling to himself.

To make the toady squirm and spill his secrets, blub-
bering in fear…

Something to think about, Basile told himself and turned back to the crackling radio.

Zona Industriale I, Calabria

UNDER NORMAL CIRCUMSTANCES, Gianni Magolino considered the drive from Catanzaro to Tropea a relaxing distraction.

His home away from home was not located in Tropea proper but a short kilometer outside of town, atop a hillside with a grand view of the sea. He'd taken Mariana there on several occasions to unwind, and they'd enjoyed themselves.

This time, she would not be so fortunate.

It had been tempting to just kill her and be done with it, but once the damned American became involved, it raised too many questions. How had he appeared so serendipitously, aiding her escape from execution? Had she been conspiring with her brother all along?

Before she died at last, he would have answers.

And revenge.

He'd phoned ahead to the doctor—not a pleasant man, but useful in a situation such as this one. He was twisted, certainly, and Magolino would have said his bedside manner was garbage, but he did the work required of him without complaint. In fact, he seemed to enjoy it, most particularly when the subject was a nubile creature such as Mariana.

What a waste! Magolino thought. If her brother had been loyal, she would have faced no danger. Even then, however, she should still have done the honorable thing, accepted his decision to eliminate her without raising all this fuss and bringing strangers into it.

The shame was hers, not Magolino's. He would make her understand soon enough.

It would not be like old times, but he might enjoy it all the same.

Magolino palmed his walkie-talkie as he spoke to the car behind his. "Any sign that we've been followed so far?"

"None, *padrino*."

"Very well," Magolino said. "Stay alert."

"Affirmative."

One good thing about the coastal drive: they should have ample opportunity to spot a tail and deal with it in the open country, without interference from police or witnesses. It might be convenient if the damned American did chase after him. They could settle their dispute like men, leaving more time for Magolino to enjoy his final hours with Mariana.

Or, the mobster thought, *he might kill us.*

It was certainly unnerving how a single man—if he was truly on his own—had carved a bloody swath through Magolino's territory, striking where and when he chose, as if impervious to harm. And then, as they were pulling out of Catanzaro, Magolino had received the first phone call reporting other outrages, these traceable, he thought, to Don Peppino Lanza.

Piece of shit!

If the Mafia chose this time to attack him, thinking Magolino had gone soft, that he was reeling from the injuries he'd suffered, they were in for a surprise.

They would regret that choice when they were drowning in their own life's blood.

Via Nuova, Catanzaro

"A CAPTAIN?" PIETRO NARDI ASKED. "You want me to lie to your captain? I don't understand, Lieutenant."

The all-night café near Villa Margherita was almost deserted. A weary waitress was sharing it with one man at the counter while Nardi sat at a corner table with Lieutenant Carlo Albanesi. The little weasel was a drug dealer and thief who occasionally served as one of Albanesi's confidential informants to earn extra money or keep himself out of Catanzaro's overcrowded prison.

"You don't need to understand it," Albanesi said, leaning toward Nardi till the round edge of the table pressed into his stomach. "All you need to do is follow orders."

"But a captain... I don't know. If anything goes wrong..."

"Remember the cocaine you were carrying at your arrest last month? I have not filed that charge yet," Albanesi said, "but I can turn the papers in at any time. Is that your fourth or fifth offense?"

"Only the third!" Nardi protested.

"Never mind. You will draw the maximum, a six-year sentence, plus a fine."

"I want to help, Lieutenant, truly. But a captain...well, if he finds out...."

"He *won't* find out, I promise you," Albanesi said. "It is just a little joke, in any case."

"He won't be angry?"

"I can guarantee it."

He'll be dead, Albanesi thought, sipping coffee to shift the lump in his throat.

"Ok," the weasel said at last, as if he'd ever had a choice. "What should I say?"

"Tell him you're one of Sergeant Coppola's informants. You have important information but you can't reach him. He left the captain's name and number to be used in an emergency."

"What if the captain checks with this sergeant?" Nardi asked.

"He can't. The sergeant is on holiday in France. You see, I've thought of everything."

"I guess so."

"There is no guessing to it," Albanesi hissed at him.

"And what about the meeting?" Nardi asked.

"Idiot! There is no meeting! All you do is call, and then forget about it, if you know what's good for you."

"No meeting?" Nardi's aspect brightened. "I misunderstood."

As usual, Albanesi thought. The lieutenant forced a smile and said, "You see? There's nothing to it."

"But my name…'

"Make up a name, for the love of— He'll never know the difference."

"Ah, now I see. What should I tell him that's so important?"

"No details," Albanesi said. "You don't trust the telephone."

"That's true enough," Nardi agreed.

Ignoring him, the officer pressed on. "Tell him you have information about Mariana. Got it? Perhaps say you know where she is."

"Mariana?"

"Don't worry about it. He'll know what you mean."

"So, I know where she is?"

"And you know it's worth money."

"But he won't be paying me?"

"Because the two of you will never meet, Pietro. Remember?"

"Oh, right. And that's all? What if he starts to ask questions?"

"Just give him the address and hang up the phone."

"Suppose he tries to trace it?" Nardi asked.

"Don't use your own phone, idiot."

"Ah." Embarrassed, Nardi flashed a nervous smile and chuckled at his own stupidity.

"And the address where I'm supposed to meet him?"

Albanesi rattled off a number on Via Vittorio Butera, waiting while Nardi repeated it.

"You have it, then? No other questions?"

"Um…"

"What is it now?"

"As for my payment…"

"Is your freedom not enough?"

"A man must eat, Lieutenant. He must pay the rent."

Despite his show of anger, Albanesi had expected this. He slid an envelope across the narrow table separating them.

"Two hundred euros, not a penny more. Fail me in this, Pietro, and the prison door will slam behind your scrawny ass before you know what's happening."

"Don't worry. It's simple, as you explained it."

"Just keep it that way, and you'll come out all right."

Albanesi tossed money on the table for their coffee, and left Nardi sitting by himself. The little worm would do as he was told, and when his job was done, no one would see his ugly face again. Another miserable dealer wouldn't be missed.

But a captain?

Albanesi thought that might turn out to be a different story altogether.

Via Azaria Tedeschi, Catanzaro

ALDO ADAMO OCCUPIED the penthouse of the Hotel Gualtier, a five-star establishment renowned for its fine service and cuisine. It offered privacy, convenience and a measure of security—although tonight, nothing would save the Magolino *cosche*'s underboss.

Bolan entered the hotel through a side door and crossed a deserted cocktail lounge, thereby avoiding the lobby staff. He wore a slouch hat to conceal his features, more or less, from the CCTV cameras he assumed were covering the corridors and elevators. On his way to the service stairs, he encountered one guest and one maid. Neither spared him more than a passing glance, dressed as he was in reasonable style, his Spectre M4 submachine gun and grenades concealed beneath his raincoat.

Bolan chose the stairs on the off chance that Adamo's soldiers had their own CCTV installed and were watching the elevator traffic. Meeting defenders on the top floor of the hostelry was one thing; being trapped inside a steel box while they riddled it with lead was something else.

On the top floor, Bolan took a moment to peer through the fire door's double-glazed, wire-mesh window into an empty hallway. When he'd satisfied himself that no ambush was waiting in the corridor, he left the stairwell, SMG in hand, and started toward the entrance to the penthouse.

He approached the door directly, head down for the cameras, and hit the dead bolt with a short burst from his Spectre, kicking through to find himself inside a large, unoccupied living room. Bolan swept the other rooms in seconds flat, found no one home, then spent another moment pondering where he might find Gianni Magolino. Stony Man's intel had given him a working list of 'Ndrangheta properties in Catanzaro and environs, but continuing to hit them in a search for *il padrino* meant a long slog for results that might be minimal at best.

Retreating hastily before hotel security showed up, he focused on the new game: finding Magolino's hideout and discovering whether his prisoner was still alive.

Two likely sources came to mind, and Bolan flipped a mental coin while he was jogging down the stairs. One or the other might be useful, and he should have time to check them both.

But could the lady still afford to wait? Or was she dead already?

Rescue mission or revenge?

Bolan could play it either way, and neither was a healthy prospect for the Magolino family.

Via della Lacina, Catanzaro

DON PEPPINO LANZA loved to hear the screams of dying enemies, but time was running short now and he had no more of it to waste on personal amusement.

"I will ask you one last time," he told the bloody ruin of a man who lay before him duct-taped to a tabletop. "If you cannot tell me where your *padrino* has run off to, I will feed you your left eye, then the right and then your testicles. So, what shall it be?"

His men had snatched the young *'ndranghetisto* from a brothel near Nicola Ceravolo Stadium on Catanzaro's north side. They had planned on burning the place after gunning down two of its guards, but the third had fumbled with his weapon and they'd taken him alive instead of running up the body count. Lanza had thanked the team leader for his initiative and made a mental note to authorize a bonus for him in his next month's salary.

Assuming the prisoner proved useful.

So far, he had stonewalled like a good soldier, but Lanza had a talent when it came to reading men, especially when they'd reached their breaking point. The young *'ndranghetisto* had resisted bravely, but his strength was failing now, draining his will to sacrifice himself for a *padrino* who would let him die without a second thought.

"No answer?" Lanza prodded. "Very well. The left eye first, as promised."

Picking up the scalpel, he leaned closer to his victim. Lanza wore a plastic jumpsuit to prevent his clothes from being stained. His blood-flecked rubber gloves were blue, making his hands look like an alien's. His goggles and his paper mask—a nod to AIDS, MERS and so many other viruses in these unhealthy times—itched where they pressed into his forehead and stubbled cheeks.

Peppino pried the youngster's eyelids open with his left hand, scalpel poised above the rolling eyeball. When punctured, Lanza knew, it would release a mini-torrent of transparent, gelatinous fluid known as the aqueous humor—though he suspected his patient would not be laughing.

Still, it never hurt to try a little levity.

"You've been a fine pupil," he told the prisoner. "I hope you'll keep an eye out for me on the other side."

His scalpel touched the shiny orb, unleashing spasms in the young man's body, which thrashed so hard Lanza briefly feared he might rip through the duct tape. At the same time, he began to babble in a high-pitched, girlish tone.

"Please, please, sir! Stop! I'll tell you what you wish to know! I swear!"

And there it was: the breaking point.

Lanza withdrew the scalpel from his prisoner's undamaged eye. "So, tell me," he commanded. "Where may I locate Gianni Magolino, the man who left you to your lonely fate?"

"Tropea!" gasped the weeping captive. "He goes there on holiday sometimes or when he needs to get away from Catanzaro for a while."

"Where in Tropea?"

"Not in town. A short kilometer or two outside, southwest, atop a hill."

"How many men are with him?" Lanza asked.

"He took a dozen in two vehicles. Some others stay there all the time to watch the place."

"That's all?"

The young man shook his head, sweat flying. "No, sir. He has called in every man available."

"But left you and the other two at his whorehouse?"

"As guards. He still has business in the city to protect from the American."

"Ah. What do you know of this American?"

"Only his name. I mean, the name he uses. No one thinks it is legitimate."

"And that name would be…?"

"Scott Parker. Please, sir. That's all I know."

Lanza stared into those panic-crazed eyes and felt himself relax. "I believe you, my son," he replied.

The scalpel drew a crimson line across the young *'ndranghetisto*'s pulsing throat, severing both carotid arteries, both jugular veins and his windpipe in one sweeping stroke. Aerated blood shot toward the ceiling, spraying Lanza's goggles, mask and plastic suit. He stepped back from the table, wondering if he would need a shower now in spite of the protective gear. A brief inspection revealed that he would only have to wipe some errant droplets from his face.

Time saved, in which he could stalk Gianni Magolino and pay his enemy back for the insult of bombing Lanza's home.

With luck, the godfather's fate would be neither as swift nor as relatively peaceful as the death of his young soldier. Lanza hoped to keep his enemy alive and screaming for at least two days.

A week would please him more, but he'd always been a relatively modest man.

11

Via Alcide de Gasperi, Catanzaro

Bolan parked at gas station to call Peppino Lanza. He got through on his first attempt and heard the *mafioso* say, "Ah, my friend! I did not have a chance to thank you for the warning earlier."

"I had a feeling you were busy," Bolan said.

"And you were right! But now I thank you, even if the warning came too late."

"You're still alive and kicking, though."

"Yes, as are you. Kicking an enemy we have in common, I believe."

"You worked that out yourself?"

"It was not difficult. Who else would be tormenting Magolino, other than the two of us?"

"That's why I'm calling," Bolan said. "If you still want to thank me for the heads up…"

"Within reason, certainly," Lanza replied.

"I just left Magolino's penthouse," Bolan told him. "You can scratch it off your list. Nobody's home."

"Indeed. I have discovered that from a cooperative member of his *cosche* only recently. And now you hope to learn where he has gone, eh?"

"Thought it might be worth a try," Bolan replied.

Lanza was silent for a moment, then said, "And why not? The enemy of my enemy, eh?"

"Sounds good to me," Bolan said.

"He's in Tropea. Do you know it?"

"I can find it."

"Magolino has a house there, on a hill outside the town, I'm told."

"And he's supposed to be there now?"

"Or on his way. I hope to see him soon, but if you find him first, may the best man win."

I plan to, Bolan thought. "Maybe I'll see you there."

"Ah. A little something extra to anticipate. How will I know you?" Lanza asked.

"Shouldn't be a problem," Bolan answered. "If you make it, I'll find you."

"And shall we still be great friends?"

"Nothing lasts forever," Bolan said.

"How true. How sad, eh? Till we meet then. Possibly in hell."

The line went dead, and Bolan set his sat phone on the empty seat beside him. Now, before he made another move, he had to ask himself if Lanza could be trusted for directions to Magolino's hideout. There was no doubt in his mind that Lanza wanted Magolino dead, and Lanza would rather do the job himself. It appeared he was accepting Bolan's first call as an honest warning, rather than an act of misdirection, but he might just as easily try cleaning house, ridding himself of Bolan at the same time as he dealt with Magolino.

Why not?

No *mafioso* ever made it to the top by trusting others, even in a close-knit family. Survival of the fittest was the basic law for predators, whether they occupied a city or a rain forest. Even if Lanza looked on Bolan as a momentary friend, eliminating him still made good sense in the long term. Who wanted foreigners lurking around and meddling in their business anyway?

So, should he make the side trip to Tropea or ignore Lanza's advice?

Captain Basile might be able to enlighten Bolan, but if tipped off to Magolino's possible location, he could lead a rescue mission of his own. The last thing Bolan needed, if the lead to Magolino proved legit, was lawmen getting underfoot and in his life of fire.

But there was always Stony Man.

A long shot, granted, but it could be worth a try.

He didn't bother calculating time zones as he picked up the sat phone once more and dialed. Someone would be awake and on the job.

They always were.

Tropea

RAF DONDINI DID not like guard duty ordinarily, but after prowling Catanzaro all night long, then driving to Tropea, it was good to stretch his legs. The property surrounding Magolino's country home sprawled over fifty acres from the hilltop at its center, and the workout Dondini got, trudging over its slopes and gullies, had his heart thumping against his ribs.

Daylight was breaking now, and soldiers were arriving in response to Magolino's call for reinforcements. Dondini could not guess how many of the family's four hundred soldiers—or, at least, the ones still living—would appear to stand with their *padrino,* but he guessed as many as a quarter of them might be close enough to make the trip on short notice. A hundred guns could make a crucial difference against their enemy, who seemed to strike from nowhere, like some kind of deadly poltergeist.

Dondini was not superstitious. He didn't believe in hexes, curses or the like, but *something* had been setting his nerves on edge. First, Rinaldo Natale had betrayed the family, violating his oath of silence, and now Natale's sister was immersed in some foul treachery. She would be punished for it soon, a show Dondini hoped he would be privileged to witness, but they still had to find the damned American known as Scott Parker—find him and prevent him from inflicting any further damage on the family.

As to the other raids in Catanzaro—starting in the hours prior to their departure and involving men who sounded very much like members of the Mafia—Dondini had no clue how that feud would resolve itself. No one consulted him on matters that pertained to policy. They only issued orders: go here, go there, kill him, kidnap her.

Do as you're told.

A soldier's life.

The walkie-talkie on his belt crackled with the hourly check-in. Aldo, at the big house, was not taking any chances. Dondini palmed the radio and simply said, "Number six."

"Confirmed," Aldo answered, then clicked off.

The rifle Dondini carried on a shoulder sling seemed to be getting heavier. That was impossible, he realized, a trick spawned by fatigue. Still, he would make it through his three-hour shift then pass the weapon and the duty to someone fresh while he went in to have a meal and catch his first sleep since the trouble had begun—how long ago? Less than a day, in fact, although it felt much longer.

How many of his brothers had been slain within that time? Dondini started counting then gave up. He'd been too busy to keep track of all the incidents, much less who was killed or wounded in each one.

Soldiers could always be replaced, as Dondini knew very well. The more important thing was getting rid of the 'ndrina's enemies in a way that helped enhance the family's reputation.

Dondini hoped he might be the one to deal with Scott Parker personally. Though it seemed unlikely, he would relish taking out a major foe while advancing himself in the process.

And the first step in that process was to stay on full alert.

Dondini slipped his automatic rifle off its shoulder sling and held it ready as he walked his beat. There was no realistic prospect of a confrontation yet, but he would not be taken by surprise.

A single shot could put him on the road to fame and fortune.

Conversely, it could put him in the ground.

San Pietro Lametino, Calabria

BOLAN MADE GOOD time southbound on the A3 Motorway, holding the Fiat Panda to the highway's posted maximum speed. He enjoyed the open road, its traffic sparse by comparison to Catanzaro's downtown snarl of cars, trucks, motorcycles and pedestrians, who often seemed intent on suicide.

He rolled the windows down and let the rush of cool air clear his head as he focused on the problem waiting for him in Tropea. Magolino would be busy circling the wagons, rallying his troops from near and far, trying to make sense of the double hits he'd been taking around Catanzaro. If he had anything resembling common sense, he must have figured out that "Scott Parker" wasn't his only active enemy. Peppino Lanza's *mafiosi* had been snapping at his heels, and now—as Bolan knew, but Magolino might not—Lanza knew where he was hiding.

It was a race to the finish line, with Mariana Natale's life in the balance.

And the odds, as usual, were heavily against the Executioner.

He stopped for fuel on the outskirts of town. Back on the road, he ran through the directions he'd received from Stony Man and confirmed the details on his laptop. Bolan had seen a satellite photo of the mobster's home away from home, and he'd begun making plans for his attack.

Preliminary only, mind you. If he reached Magolino's hilltop retreat and found it crawling with 'Ndrangheta soldiers armed to the teeth, his plan would need some tweaking, maybe radical revision. Any way you sliced it, the bottom line was penetration, followed by a search for Mariana if the circumstances made that feasible. That was a big "if," Bolan realized, and it was followed by another: finding out if she was still alive and fit to travel, or if she would need a medevac to get her off the property. The latter option meant involving the authorities, killing as many *'ndranghetisti* as he could before help arrived, then leaving Mariana in official hands while he escaped.

If that was even feasible.

Long odds? Try verging on impossible.

But he was bound to try.

Chinese tradition, as he understood it, said that if you saved another person's life, you were obliged to care for them from that day forward. Bolan didn't buy that, but he *did* believe he was responsible for Mariana in the here and now. If he wrote her off, it was the same as if he'd never helped her in the first place, and his private code of honor wouldn't let him live with that.

Choices.

Each battle threw a thousand of them at a fighting man, and Bolan was no stranger to split-second decisions made under fire. Today, he would be going up against the 'Ndrangheta for two reasons: first, to save one life a second time; and second, to impart a lesson that survivors of the outlaw "family" would take to heart.

And he'd be doing it in broad daylight, rather than wasting twelve more hours—letting Mariana suffer, maybe die—while he waited for the sun to set.

A high-noon blitz. Full speed ahead.

Tropea

THE TORTURE HAD not started yet, but it was coming. Mariana Natale knew that as surely as she knew she would never leave this place alive.

Her mood shifted erratically from one moment to the next, veering between outraged defiance and abject terror, accompanied by tremors she could not seem to control. Raised in the 'Ndrangheta tradition, she knew well enough the kinds of punishment reserved for traitors, death being the least of them. A part of her hoped she could stay strong in the face of unimaginable agony and degradation, cursing her tormentors to the bloody end, but Mariana had her doubts.

She had considered suicide, hellfire be damned, but her hands and feet were securely bound. Beyond that, she had scanned her tiny room as best she could—from her position on its narrow single bed—and saw nothing that could have served her as a weapon, even if her hands were free to wield one. Suffocation would not work; the human brain refused to let its host stop breathing voluntarily and would resume that function on its own, even if she persisted long enough to cause unconsciousness.

Likewise, her bonds prevented Mariana from inflicting any lethal harm upon herself without an instrument of some kind. At the worst, she could roll out of bed and try to pound her head against the floor, but it was thickly carpeted, so unlikely to do more than add a headache to her present physical and mental suffering.

Hopeless.

She was at Magolino's mercy, and he did not understand the meaning of the word.

That left two options: the defiance she'd considered previously or a groveling plea for her life that she knew would be useless. Why humiliate herself for Gianni's amusement?

Defiance it was, then, as long as she could make it last. At some point, Mariana knew, she would become a screaming mass of violated flesh, devoid of reason, praying—if she still remembered how to pray—for death's release. No human being could withstand torture indefinitely, even if it seemed to happen frequently in Hollywood films.

She'd break, all right. And it would make no difference.

Gianni did not plan to simply punish her. He wanted to *destroy* her by the slowest and most agonizing means he could devise.

A wave of nausea passed over Mariana and left her weak and trembling as she played the blame game. Who was responsible for her predicament? Rinaldo, for betraying Magolino when he turned informer in New York? Their parents, who had raised them to regard the 'Ndrangheta as a law unto itself, guided by "honor," which she knew to be a hollow sham?

Or was the fault entirely hers?

Only her brother was expected to pursue their father's criminal profession. Girls were not pressured to find gainful employment, educate themselves beyond the basics or do anything past finding a husband and raising a family. It had been Mariana's choice to chase the high life among Rinaldo's cronies, and it had led her to Gianni Magolino.

It had led her here.

With that knowledge, her despair returned in full force. Knowing she could expect no help, she closed her eyes and wept.

Pizzo, Calabria

PEPPINO LANZA GLANCED through the tinted window of his limo toward the sea, but he failed to register its beauty. He was not a great sightseer, never had been, and today of all days was no time for him to start appreciating scenery.

The sea was *there;* it always had been and would always be there. So, what of it?

Lanza's problem, now, was getting through the next few hours with his skin and fighting force intact. He had strict orders from the leaders of the Bevilacqua family in Palermo—redeem himself or die in the attempt. No third alternative was either contemplated or permissible.

No problem, Lanza told himself. His task was simple when you thought about it: storm a fortified redoubt with twenty-odd soldiers, against what he presumed must be a vastly larger force of better-armed defenders, kill them all and thereby save his reputation from complete annihilation.

Simple.

Every weapon he possessed was packed into the four-car caravan proceeding toward Tropea. If they happened to be stopped by the police, he'd given orders to try bribery first, then let the chips fall where they would. Lanza would not permit the cops to divert him from his mission or his destiny, whatever that might prove to be.

His secret weapon was the brash American, assuming he took the bait and rushed off to Tropea. Any injury inflicted on the 'Ndrangheta would help Lanza, and if the wildman decimated Magolino's troops, so much the better. Dealing with a single enemy, or a handful of stunned survivors, would be preferable to a gangland replay of Gallipoli, with Lanza and his soldiers cast as the Australians.

Lanza could not see himself in the Mel Gibson role, no matter how he squinted at his bathroom mirror.

Ugly little gargoyle. Lanza's wife had called him that after imbibing too much wine shortly before she had had

her accident. Even a drunken woman should know better
than to keep a hair dryer plugged in and resting on a bathroom counter near the tub where she enjoyed her ninety-
minute bubble baths. The marble tub had definitely been
a *hot* tub that day, and if anyone asked Lanza, he would
have to say replacing the bathroom's burned-out wall socket
ranked among his best investments ever.

Back to business.

Every soldier in his service was riding with Lanza
toward what might be their last great hurrah. He'd also
phoned Palermo to report his plan, in case it all went wrong.
Don Bevilacqua could decide what action was required, if
any, after Lanza and his men were shoveled under. Maybe
he would pull out of Calabria entirely, making all of it an
exercise in sheer futility.

But that would not be Lanza's concern.

Win or lose, live or die, his problem with Gianni Magolino would be solved today.

An old Sicilian proverb said *Sangue lava sangue*. Blood
washes blood. That might not always be the case, but in the
present circumstance, blood-letting was required.

The only question now was whether Lanza and his men
were equal to the task.

Tropea

ON THE TOWN'S OUTSKIRTS, Bolan slowed to match the pace
of traffic. He drove southwestward through what passed
for suburbs in a smallish coastal town then back into open
country as he left the tourist traps behind.

Five minutes more and Bolan's hilltop target was visible, lording over the landscape like a feudal manor house.
The view from Magolino's third-floor balcony must be fan-
tastic, but Bolan hadn't come to ogle scenery or shop for
souvenirs. Bolan would chart the best daylight approach,

merging his on-site observations with the details on his laptop, and plot his entry to the hostile property.

A fortress now, beyond much doubt.

A fortress *and* a prison.

Allowing for the possibility of CCTV cameras on the walls surrounding Magolino's grounds, Bolan drove past, resisting any urge to dawdle, and continued on a mile until another hill blocked any view of where he'd leave the car. He was fortunate to find an access road nearly overgrown with weeds—which proved it was rarely used—that led him off the provincial road a hundred yards or so to reach a shady copse of trees.

He parked there and waited, listening and watching for a sign of human life in the vicinity, but none was evident. Ten minutes crept past on his watch before he stirred, climbed from the car and started changing clothes.

No night gear for a daylight probe, but he had forest camos with him and made the switch in nothing flat. He'd seen that Magolino's grounds were wooded, though the trees had been clear-cut for twenty yards or so around the looming house. He would take full advantage of the terrain as long as possible, and after that...

Well, he would simply have to see what happened.

Chaos and bloodshed, in a nutshell, but the way it unfolded was unique to every skirmish, every battle, every great campaign. He was prepared to improvise, adapt and soldier on, no matter what went down once battle had been joined.

For this round, Bolan carried every weapon he'd purchased in Calabria. He wore the ARX across his back and carried the silent Spectre M4. His Beretta 93R was slung in armpit leather, while the ebony-handled stiletto went into a cargo pocket of his pants. Weighed down with ammo magazines, a bandolier of 40 mm rounds and all his remaining frag grenades, he might have rattled when he walked, except that all the gear was well secured.

Was he a dead man walking or grim death itself?

The next hour or so would tell.

Trees, gullies and boulders on the landward side of Magolino's property covered the Executioner on his approach. The mile and change he covered, most of it uphill, would have been daunting for a sometime weekend hiker, but it proved no challenge for a man who kept himself in fighting trim year-round. The trick, in fact, was going slow enough to watch his step, wary of traps set for potential trespassers and cameras or other gear that may have been installed on the perimeter.

Time might be running out for Mariana—if she wasn't dead already—but it wouldn't help her if he walked into an ambush before he reached Gianni Magolino's rural palace. She would have to wait a little longer, bear a little more, before her knight in camo armor made his final move.

Make that the final move for Magolino and his family.

The only end Bolan allowed himself to contemplate.

12

Via Vittorio Butera, Catanzaro

Captain Basile parked his unmarked car a block from the café his anonymous caller had specified. He sat behind the wheel, watching foot traffic on the street. No passing pedestrian looked any more or less suspicious than the next; none of the cars parked up and down the street seemed to be occupied.

What am I doing here? Basile asked himself not for the first time since he'd received the breathless call.

It was a measure of his desperation, he supposed—and his guilt at failing Mariana Natale and the friends who'd died defending her. Basile knew he was grasping at straws and understood the anonymous call was most likely a hoax or a trap, but what else could he do?

I could have brought backup, he thought, but the caller had insisted he come alone or lose his opportunity to rescue Mariana. It was madness, plain and simple, taking orders from a stranger on the telephone, but he'd felt compelled to roll the dice. For Mariana and himself.

Or maybe I'm just tired of living, he considered, shrugging off the morbid thought a second later. Stepping from the car, Basile reached inside his jacket, adjusting the thumb break holster where his Beretta 84BB nestled snugly. In addition to the pistol, he carried a steel telescoping baton that would extend from six to eighteen inches with a flick of his wrist.

Not much, perhaps, but he'd done his best. Taking the shotgun from his Fiat Bravo's trunk would only cause a panic on the street and frighten off his contact. If there *was* a contact.

Stupid, said the small voice in Basile's head. *Call backup.*

He ignored it and struck off toward the café. When no one intercepted him, Basile chose a sidewalk table, ordered coffee and prepared to wait. It gave him one more chance to scan the street and check its overhanging windows, looking for a sniper or some sign he was being watched. Other than the fact that he was there alone and waiting for a stranger to approach him, nothing seemed out of place.

His waiter brought the coffee and retreated. As Basile sipped it, he observed two men emerging from a shop across the street, both broken-nose types, most unlikely to be browsing the establishment's racks of maternity wear. Sweeping his eyes along the street, he saw another pair of thugs exit a copy shop that doubled as an Internet café.

Damn! He had, as feared, walked straight into a trap.

But set by whom?

Basile drew his pistol and held it in his lap, his index finger curled around the double-action trigger. Sipping coffee with his left hand, he pretended not to see the goons advancing on him in a pincer movement, crossing the street against traffic while horns blared around them.

So subtle.

It was difficult, pretending to be blind and stupid—though, indeed, he felt that way. His mind raced as he tried to decide who'd set him up, always returning to a single suspect.

Carlo Albanesi.

Who else would—

Basile raised his gun and fired when the gorillas on his left were twenty feet away. His first shot ripped into a flabby, stubbled cheek and rocked the target on his heels. Basile shifted for his next round, putting a .380 ACP bullet near center of mass on the first man's hulking companion.

Down, now!

Basile tipped his table, diving to the pavement as the shooters on his right pulled guns and opened fire. Their first rounds were too high, but they kept trying, steadily advancing. Aiming through a knee-high wrought-iron fence that framed the café's outdoor dining area, Basile shot one of them in the thigh and saw his thick leg buckle, spouting blood. The shooter fell, cursing, but tried to fire again until Basile's fourth round clipped one of his yellow peg incisors, blowing out the back of his skull.

Number four was getting desperate, shouting and blazing away, his bullets cracking off concrete and metal chairs around the spot where Basile lay cringing. Swallowing his fear, Basile sent a double-tap down range, drilling the final gunman's groin and setting loose an eerie howl of pain. Basile's seventh shot silenced the wailing, then he turned back toward the face-shot goon he'd wounded first.

The man was breathing raggedly, blowing wet crimson bubbles through the vent in his right cheek. He might be dying, but Basile could not tell and didn't care. He palmed his cell phone to report the shooting and began rehearsing how he would explain the incident.

Before he went to find a certain lieutenant.

Tropea

BOLAN PAUSED AT the tree line, still hidden by shadows, to check out the wall surrounding Magolino's property. He saw no CCTV cameras, but with surveillance gear today, a fiber-optic fish-eye lens could watch him from a tiny hole drilled through one of the cinder blocks. Another option would be cameras directed from the hilltop house, but Bolan thought the wooded grounds would interfere too much with spying from a distance.

He would take advantage of those trees—but first, he had to cross some thirty yards of open ground and scale the eight-foot wall.

He had two options for the last few yards of his approach: rush to the wall, or take it slow and easy. Bolan knew it wouldn't matter if a camera had spotted him; observers would be tracking him whether he ran or crawled. But if there was no camera…

He thought of Mariana as he broke from cover, springing through bright sunshine to the shade of Magolino's outer wall. Bolan angled toward a spot where trees grew thick on the inside of the barrier, obstructing the view from the big house. Sheltered there, he waited for another moment, just to see if any guards came swarming out to meet him. When they didn't, he prepared to climb.

Slinging the M4 SMG over his shoulder, Bolan leaped to catch the topmost row of cinder blocks, hoisted himself onto the rough concrete and lay prone while he got a closer look at Magolino's grounds than any satellite could offer.

First, he looked for guards and dogs but spotted neither. Before that changed, he dropped over the side, landed in a fighting crouch and unslung the Spectre, ready for whatever challenge might present itself.

His next problem was getting to the house itself and then making his way inside—assuming he could do all that without meeting at least a few of Magolino's men. His M4 and Beretta offered quiet ways of dealing with the property's defenders, but he couldn't count on any of their weapons being silenced, and it took only one shot—one shout—to bring the full weight of the home team down on top of him.

And so far, Bolan didn't even know how many soldiers he was up against.

One more thing he would have to learn before it was too late.

Guardia di Finanza Headquarters

LIEUTENANT ALBANESI FELT a prickling on his scalp as he half whispered into his cell phone, "What? Who blew it?"

"How should I know who they were?" Pietro Nardi replied. "The men you sent to do it."

"I sent no one," Albanesi hissed. "Remember that!"

"Whatever. *Someone* sent them, and they screwed it up. All four of them are dead."

At that, the phone almost escaped from Albanesi's sweaty, trembling hand.

"He killed four?"

"As I said. I saw it happen."

"Shit!" Albanesi had believed it would be easy to remove Captain Basile from the picture. He'd left the dirty work to Magolino's men after the trap was baited, but he'd obviously been mistaken. Now...

"And he escaped unharmed?"

"Without a scratch," Nardi replied. "Maybe he got a little dusty, rolling on the sidewalk."

"Did he see you?"

Nardi thought about it for a moment, then replied. "Impossible. I watched it from a block away."

"And the police are there?"

"Like flies on shit. I'm getting out of town."

"No, wait—" But he was gone, the dial tone blowing its raspberry into Albanesi's ear. "Bastard!"

He was getting nowhere, cursing empty air, so Albanesi put his phone away and left his claustrophobic office, heading for the elevators and the underground garage. His plan to get rid of Basile had been desperate, fueled by the captain's obvious suspicion, but the scheme had blown up in his face. How long before Basile came for him or sent a flying squad of officers to start interrogating Albanesi?

He's got nothing, the lieutenant told himself, but it rang hollow. The shooters might be dead, and Nardi was leaving town, but once Basile got a notion in his head, he couldn't let it go. If he was after Albanesi now...

How would it happen, if they met at headquarters? Basile was a stickler for procedure—what the Americans called a "straight arrow"—but if he thought Albanesi had plotted to kill him, would he lose control? Albanesi was younger but hardly in shape for a brawl with a madman, and if he pulled a gun on Basile in front of their fellow officers, he might as well present the prosecutor with a signed confession.

Which would be irrelevant if he was dead.

He reached the elevator without being intercepted and whipped out his phone after the doors closed. A voice he did not recognize answered Aldo Adamo's phone.

"What?"

Albanesi identified himself and said, "I need to speak with him."

"He's not here."

"Where has he gone?"

"Tropea, with the others."

Damnation! Albanesi cut the link without responding and pocketed his phone as he arrived in the garage. What should he do? Who would protect him now?

His only hope had been Magolino, gone to ground now in Tropea. Albanesi saw his only option laid before him. It meant leaving everything—his home, his job, his life, such as it was—but if he stayed in Catanzaro, what was left to him? Arrest, disgrace and prison. Likely death, when Magolino realized the weak lieutenant might betray him.

No. A show of loyalty to his *padrino* might go far toward

saving Albanesi in his darkest hour. And if not, it simply meant death would find him that much sooner.

Either way, Albanesi thought, he would be out of his misery.

Tropea

ONE OF PEPPINO LANZA's men had scouted Magolino's country hideout weeks ago, preparing for a strike in case the opportunity arose. He'd reported that the house and grounds seemed pretty well secured, a high-risk target unless Lanza could assemble overwhelming forces. That was not the case today, but never mind.

Lanza was running out of time.

The road to Magolino's country mansion offered no concealment, but Lanza had a plan to compensate for that. He'd called ahead and rented two delivery vans, each large enough to carry half his men in back and heavy enough— he hoped—to ram their way through Magolino's wrought-iron gates. Once they were in, the rest came down to raw audacity and fighting spirit, both of which his men had in abundance.

And, of course, it would not hurt if they could catch a break.

Lanza went through the motions of examining both vans, leaving his two appointed drivers to examine what was underneath their hoods. He was not mechanical, beyond some skill at field stripping a gun, and saw no benefit to learning now that he had skilled subordinates.

His hasty plan would either work or it would not. In one case, he would be a hero to the Bevilacqua family; in the other, he would be a corpse. There was no in-between.

At least if it went badly, Lanza knew he would not die alone.

"All ready?" Lanza asked his drivers when they finished checking out the trucks. One simply nodded, while the other said, "They'll do, *padrino*."

Lanza removed a wad of euros from his pocket, gave it to the rental agent and waited, none too patiently, as they were counted. When he was satisfied, the other man asked Lanza, "They will be returned in good condition, eh?"

"Certainly. In good condition," Lanza said, "or not at all?"

Now the rental agent wore a worried look.

"A little joke, my friend," Lanza replied. "Your property is sacrosanct to me."

What was another lie, after the thousands—maybe millions—he'd told? The trucks would likely be abandoned, shot to hell, perhaps with Lanza's bullet-riddled body. Either way, the agent did not have his true name or address, and if he tried to follow up with legal action, he would run head-on into the Bevilacqua family.

The ultimate dead end.

"Load up!" Lanza commanded, and his men began climbing into the cargo vans. Some of their weapons showed, as they got in, and that was fine. It would intimidate the rental agent and, if he was wise, ensure his silence, come what may. Calabrians were almost as inured to syndicated crime as were Sicilians, raised to understand *omertà* and the cost of speaking out of turn.

His men were quickly stowed away. Lanza considered joining half the team in the first truck's cargo compartment, then decided it would look like cowardice. He took the empty seat beside his driver, feeling bulkier than usual in a Kevlar vest. It would do nothing to protect his face from bullets coming through the windshield, but, he thought, you can't have everything.

Unless he managed to survive the coming fight and bring Gianni Magolino's head back to Salerno. In that case, Lanza believed, he just might have it all.

BOLAN MOVED THROUGH the trees like a ghost. He was on full alert for traps, security devices or patrolling guards. After he'd covered thirty yards, he was convinced no one had seen him scale the outer wall and was puzzled and pleased by Magolino's failure to install some manner of high-tech defenses. Even guard dogs, a traditional approach in Italy, would have enhanced security, but Bolan didn't try to second-guess his adversary's failing. He would simply take advantage of it while he could.

At forty yards, he met one of the 'Ndrangheta sentries. Young and bored by the routine task, the so-called soldier had stopped to relieve himself against the trunk of a parasol pine and missed death's approach from behind. Bolan pumped a single, silent 9 mm round into his cerebellum, canceling all motor function in a heartbeat, and the dead man folded like an empty suit of clothes, his privates artlessly displayed.

After depositing his first kill in a nearby clump of shrubbery, Bolan claimed the little walkie-talkie from the corpse's belt, turned down its volume to a whisper and moved on.

If Magolino had all his sentries walking solo beats, it could be good or bad. The up side was that Bolan probably shouldn't expect to meet a squad of soldiers tromping through the woods around the manor house. The down side: he couldn't predict where he might find the next lookout, or even guess how many were deployed around the grounds.

Say Magolino had reached out to—what—a quarter of his family's troops on short notice? Of that hundred or so, how many could have reached Tropea within ninety minutes' time? Thirty to forty seemed a likely estimate, but Bolan couldn't bank on it. He'd come prepared to face an army, and if it came down to that, it wouldn't be the first time.

Or, he hoped, the last.

A blitz was one thing, but his thoughts came back to

Mariana now, as he drew closer to the big house on the hill. A floor plan would have come in handy, but he hadn't had the time or resources to comb through local records, snoop around with architects or try some other angle of attack. That meant going in blind, once the house had been breached, and using logic to determine where a prisoner was likely to be locked away.

Her captor might want privacy, depending on the punishment he had in mind, and the noise could be a factor. If his brain cells were connected, Magolino must have thought about the clean-up chores that followed executions and interrogations. Given his profession and the frequency with which he slaughtered enemies, the mansion might include a special chamber just for wet work.

In the basement, Bolan thought, *where you'd expect to find a dungeon.*

It was food for thought but useless to him if he never got inside the place.

One hundred yards without another sentry in his path, and he was halfway to the house. Already, he could pick out distant voices, members of the home team on their rounds, although he couldn't understand what they were saying. No alarms had sounded yet, and that was all that mattered right now.

Step by cautious step, he closed in on the viper's nest.

MARIANA HEARD VOICES and footsteps on concrete, outside her small basement cell. Two men, perhaps more, and she recognized one of the voices. Gianni was coming to see her, and that made her tremble with fear.

She fought to conceal it, but lying trussed up on the bed offered no hope of striking a dignified pose. She was helpless, defenseless, restricted to speaking. And what would she say? Begging for mercy was pointless and humiliating. Cursing Gianni might enrage him, prodding him to kill her quickly, but survival instincts made her hesitant to rush the end.

Shut up and listen, she decided. If Gianni wanted information, maybe she could buy some time by stringing out her answers.

Time for what? Again, she came up blank.

The door opened and Magolino entered, muttered to someone who remained outside and closed the door. He studied Mariana from a distance, face impassive, before asking, "Are you comfortable?"

"Does it matter?"

"No," he said. "But I don't want you losing feeling in your arms and legs. It spoils the entertainment, later on."

"Untie me then," she answered.

"I think not." Magolino dragged the room's one chair over to sit beside her bed, well out of spitting range. "Your nose looks painful," he observed. "I may have the doctor straighten it."

"No, thank you."

Magolino laughed at that. "We don't consult the patients in our small hospice," he said.

Hospice, not *hospital*, she noted. A facility for those who are dying.

"Perhaps he'll geld you," Mariana said.

Gianni's face darkened, but he did not lash out at her this time. "A little of the same old fire," he said. "That's good."

"I don't know what it is you hope to get from me, Gianni."

"Information, possibly. If not…at least revenge."

"For what? The only thing I did was—"

"Hold me up to ridicule!" he thundered, leaning forward, elbows on his knees, fists clenched. "Make me a laughingstock! Endanger everything I've worked for all these years!"

"One little woman? I had no idea you were so fragile."

He longed to strike her—she felt the fury simmering inside him, saw the vein pulsing at his left temple. Somehow, he managed to restrain himself and eased back in his chair.

"I loved you once," he said. "Or thought I did. Clearly, it was a serious mistake."

"You used me," she corrected him. "We used each other."

"So, we're just a pair of whores, eh?" Magolino asked her through clenched teeth.

"I may be a whore," Mariana said. "I don't know what you are."

That made him smile a predatory grin that chilled her to the bone.

"Perhaps not, Mariana. But you're going to find out." He checked his bulky, foolishly expensive watch. "Within the hour, I'll return. Your education shall begin."

She held the tears back until Magolino had departed and the door was locked behind him, then the wretched sobbing started. Mariana wept for her brother, her parents, herself. She wept for the life she'd wasted and what might have been.

Above all else, she wept for lack of hope.

13

Tropea

The second guard was better, deviating from the tiresome circuit of his beat to lie in ambush, watching for intruders. If he hadn't sneezed, he might have glimpsed Mack Bolan soon enough to save himself.

The muffled sneeze gave Bolan all the warning he required to stop in midstride, then retreat, retrace his steps and come up on the lookout's blind side. He closed the gap until he stood behind the gunman, who was crouched in turn behind a clump of hemlock, with a semiautomatic shotgun on the ground beside him.

Bolan could have rushed him and used the switchblade, but why grapple with the shooter, risking injury, when he could settle it from ten feet out? The Spectre M4 coughed again, spraying the hemlock with a gout of blood and gray matter. The dead *'ndranghetisto* lurched into the poison shrubs and hung there, suspended, as his life drained through the shattered ruin of his face.

Bolan relieved the lookout of his weapon—a Benelli Ultra Light with a sawed-off barrel—checked its load and slipped its sling over his left shoulder. The 28-gauge weapon lived up to its name, weighing in at five pounds to qualify as the world's lightest semiauto shotgun, but it packed a punch, and he reckoned it couldn't hurt to have a scattergun for backup once the stealth phase of his probe had passed.

Another hundred yards or so would bring him to the tree line, where the open ground began. Bolan no longer heard Magolino's soldiers conversing ahead of him. They might've gone back inside or moved to the far side of the mansion. Maybe they were on patrol or setting up a cook-out. Bolan neither knew nor cared as long as he could find a clear path to his goal.

He crouched behind a screen of juniper and Swiss pine, studying the mansion with its roof of barrel tiles, white stucco walls and long wings extending to the east and west. The swimming pool was to his left, an empty tennis court off to his right. Farther beyond the pool, but out of sight from his position, stood a seven-car garage. He knew there was no helipad, but he supposed the vast south lawn would serve as well without unduly ruffling anyone who might be lounging on the covered flagstone patio.

It was a lot of ground to cover, about fifty yards between the tree line and that patio, where tinted glass doors stared across the lawn like huge dark eyes. Whether they opened onto an empty or occupied parlor, dining room or rec room, Bolan had no way of knowing. For all he knew, a dozen shooters might be watching his approach, but the alternative was circling around in search of other access to the home's interior, and that might take him to the por-tico in front.

Better to take his chances from the rear and meet what-ever challenge came his way with firepower in hand. As soon as Bolan stepped out of the trees and into sunlight, he would be fair game for any mobster on the property, but he'd played that game before and walked away the winner.

This time?

Let's find out, he thought and started toward the house.

Via Eugenio di Riso, Catanzaro

"CAPTAIN! YOU SURPRISED ME," the informer said.

"I meant to, Arrigo," Captain Basile replied.

Arrigo Pecorella peered out of his small apartment's doorway, moist eyes scanning up and down the street. "Are you alone, sir?"

"No GOA today," Basile said, referring to the GDF's *Gruppo Operativo Antidroga,* the Counter-narcotics Group, which would worry a meth-head like Pecorella the most. "At least," he added, "not yet."

"What can I do for you? You know I normally deal with Lieutenant Albanesi."

"That's why I'm here," Basile said.

He had missed Albanesi at headquarters, had missed him at home and now was reduced to grilling the man's top confidential informant. Basile had no reason to believe Albanesi would inform such vermin of his travel plans, but Pecorella might be able to impart some other useful information.

"May I come in?" Basile asked.

"Well…"

Basile drew his baton, flicked it open and cracked Pecorella across the bridge of his hooked nose, slamming him backward and onto the floor. Stepping across the bleating junkie, Basile shut the door, then swung his baton again across one of Pecorella's raised elbows.

"For the love of God, Captain! What have I done?"

"You've done nothing, Arrigo, except to exist as a damned parasite. I am not here to talk about you."

"What then?"

Basile had decided the one place Albanesi might attempt to hide from him was with the 'Ndrangheta. That meant running off to find Gianni Magolino or his underboss, Aldo Adamo. As it happened, presently neither one of them could be found in Catanzaro.

"You know Gianni Magolino?" he asked Pecorella.

"I know *of* him. We don't move in the same circles, Captain."

"Different levels of the sewer. I understand. But you must have some knowledge of his whereabouts."

"I don't—"

The black baton lashed out again and made Pecorella squeal. Part of Basile's mind rebelled at the brutality; another part exulted in it. "What was that?"

"He might have left the city," Pecorella whimpered. "All the trouble recently."

"I know that much already," Basile said. "What I want to know is *where* he goes."

"A man that rich—wherever he desires." The man saw Basile raising the baton again and quickly added, "but he likes Tropea best! He has another home there. Very nice, I hear, although he has yet to invite me."

"In Tropea?"

"Well, outside the town a little way. I saw it once, just driving by. It's on a hilltop. Very elegant. You can't miss it."

"I hope you're correct," Basile said, "for your own sake."

He left then, closing and holstering the baton before he reached his waiting car. He thought about requesting backup, possibly a helicopter and an entry team from the GDF's Antiterrorism and Rapid Response unit, but he didn't know who he could trust at headquarters to organize the raid.

No, he decided. It was better if he went alone. At least assess the situation first before he asked for help.

Would Pecorella squeal to his superiors? Basile doubted it, but if that happened, he was ready to explain himself and bear responsibility. By that time, if his supervisor found him, he would either have his man in custody, with a confession, or he would be dead.

And did it matter which?

Pulling away from Pecorella's drab apartment, Basile

took a hasty inventory of his gear. He had his pistol and baton, the tired suit on his back and, in the Fiat Bravo's trunk, a Benelli M4 Tactical shotgun with a full magazine and two spare boxes of buckshot.

It sounded like a lot of firepower, but it might not get Basile very far against Lieutenant Albanesi's well-armed, lowlife friends.

Tropea

Lieutenant Carlo Albanesi—make that *ex*-lieutenant, now that he was on the run—had phoned Aldo Adamo from the outskirts of Tropea to declare he needed help. The 'Ndrangheta underboss had seemed less than sympathetic, but he'd finally given into Albanesi's begging and agreed that he could proceed to Magolino's hilltop hideaway.

Now, as he pulled up to the entrance, Albanesi wondered if he'd made a grave mistake.

If he'd angered Magolino or Adamo, even if they simply found him useless now that he'd fled Catanzaro and the GDF, would they simply dispose of him rather than offer him sanctuary? Once that thought took hold, he almost turned around and drove away, but the guards were opening tall wrought-iron gates and waving him through, and Albanesi worried *they* might kill him if he tried to cut and run.

Dejected and sick with worry that he might have trapped himself, he drove with hands clenched on the steering wheel along a curving driveway that delivered him to Magolino's broad front porch. Adamo was already waiting for him, flanked by two stout *'ndranghetisti* who resembled Russian weightlifters: no necks to speak of, massive shoulders, barrel torsos, legs like tree stumps straining at the seams of shiny suits.

Albanesi wondered if bullets would stop them and decided it made no difference.

He'd walked into the lion's den. If they were hungry, he was dead.

He switched his engine off and stepped out of the car, leaving his key in the ignition. What did he care if they stole his vehicle after they'd murdered him? It was of less importance than the sudden twitching Albanesi felt between his meaty shoulder blades, as if a blade or bullet were about to pierce him.

"Your timing's not the best, Lieutenant," Adamo said. "But since you're here, come on inside."

"I did my best," Albanesi said as they crossed the threshold into rural splendor. "I can't help it if—"

"Your captain killed four of my men," Adamo said, cutting him off. "He got away. If that's your best, I'd hate to see your worst."

"I set the meeting, as instructed," Albanesi answered, cheeks warming even as a chill ran down his spine. "What else was I supposed to do?"

"An interesting question. Possibly *observe* and make sure all went as planned?"

"He would have seen me. That Basile—"

"Or, he might have smelled your fear. You'd find it easier to hide if you lost weight."

"I was not told to do the job myself. If that had been the case—"

"I'm not the one you need to sell," Adamo interrupted him once more. "You'll see him later. He's…engaged with other business this afternoon. You'll wait."

"Of course. Captain Basile—"

"Can he trace you here?" Adamo asked. "And is he fool enough to follow you if so?"

"He may suspect I'd come to you for help. Whether that brings him to Tropea…who can say?"

"You really don't know much, do you?" Adamo mocked him.

He had no good answer to that question. Albanesi let it

pass as they arrived outside a hand-carved wooden door. "You'll wait in here," Adamo said. "The library. You read?"

Embarrassed, angry, Albanesi simply bobbed his head in the affirmative.

"Maybe you'll find something to interest you. Your dinner will be brought to you if *il padrino* is still occupied. This room has a lavatory. Do not leave the library for any reason whatsoever. Understood?"

"Yes, sir. Thank you."

"Don't thank me yet," Adamo said. "You may have nothing to be grateful for."

And he was gone, closing the door behind him and leaving Albanesi in a room where shelves of books rose to the ceiling on all sides, so tall that ladders were required to reach the higher ones.

"I read," the former lieutenant muttered to himself.

He wondered if he'd already seen the writing on the wall.

BOLAN WAS FOCUSED on his dash between the tree line and the manor house. Once he'd crossed that open ground without drawing attention to himself, he couldn't linger on the patio, exposed to any passerby or sentry traipsing through the woods.

He had to get inside.

He tried the sliding door, and it immediately opened to his touch. Why bother locking it when they were on a walled estate with guards around? The logic worked for him, but Bolan thought Gianni Magolino might regret his little lapses as the hour wore on.

Inside, a softly humming air conditioner relieved the afternoon's heat and humidity, drying the sweat on Bolan's face and neck. The rec room—he'd been right about it, playing the percentages—was empty when he entered, balls neatly racked on a green baize billiard table, electronic games on the east wall silent and dark. He moved past easy chairs and sofas to reach another door across the room.

Each step he took from there on led him deeper into Magolino's home.

Gripping the silent Spectre SMG, he listened at the door for voices but heard none. Next, Bolan cracked it, peered into the hall beyond and found it as deserted as the rec room. Bolan eased into the corridor, leaving the door ajar for a swift retreat. He had a choice of going left or right and picked left because he heard the sound of muffled voices from that direction.

Discovery, at this point, meant more killing, a warning to the other soldiers spread throughout the house and grounds. If he could find a Magolino flunky on his own, Bolan still had a chance—however slim—to reach Mariana without setting off a general alarm.

All it would take was nerve, some luck and possibly a miracle.

One soldier, on his own, as careless as his buddies in the woods had been. Was that too much to ask?

A toilet flushed behind the next door to his right. Bolan froze in his tracks and waited for the door to open, then stepped forward and pressed the Spectre's silencer against a skull covered with oily, slicked-back hair.

"Where is the woman?" Bolan asked.

"What woman?" came back to him in a squeaky, nervous voice.

"Wrong answer. Say good-bye."

"Wait! I can take you to her!"

"One more chance," Bolan told him. "Lead the way."

PEPPINO LANZA SAW the imposing gates as his truck rounded a final curve and growled its way up the hilltop in low gear. His driver kept the pedal down, fighting the grade. Their truck rocked drunkenly from side to side, making him wonder if his men were getting sick in back. If one threw up, Lanza thought, the nausea could spread like wildfire in the stuffy, claustrophobic rear compartment.

Almost there.

Lanza cradled a Beretta M12 submachine gun in his lap, drawing comfort from its solid weight across his meaty thighs. The little weapon, less than seventeen inches long with its metal stock folded, was chambered in 9 mm Parabellum. The forty-round mag he had loaded was the largest available; smaller ones, twenty and thirty-two rounds apiece, bulged from the pockets of his suit.

Today, fashion was taking a backseat to practicality. And to survival.

Two guards, both armed with automatic rifles, were eyeing Lanza's trucks as they approached. They would be suspicious, certainly, but Lanza had no reason to believe the pair would recognize him as an enemy on sight—at least, until he opened fire on them.

But first…

"Slow down and let me out," he ordered, and the driver grunted in response, downshifting and easing on the brake.

The guards were on alert as Lanza's truck rolled to a stop six feet in front of them. He smiled and waved through the windscreen, then opened his door and began to step out, shielding his submachine gun with the cab's open door.

"Hello, friends! Can you tell me if I've reached the right address?"

"Unlikely," one of them replied. "We're not expecting a delivery."

"Well, damn! Is this not the home of…just a minute, please.…"

Lanza stepped down to the pavement, then revealed his weapon, firing from the hip before they could react. Some of his bullets struck the wrought-iron scrollwork of the massive gates, but most of them passed through, whipping the guards into a jerky tarantella, blood exploding from their wounds as they collapsed onto the driveway's asphalt.

Lanza vaulted back into the truck's cab and shouted at his driver, "Go! Go!"

The truck lurched forward, struck the gate and powered through it, metal screaming as it snagged, ripped free and clawed across the fenders, doors and cargo van behind. Lanza was worried for a moment that they might stick fast, block the opening and get trapped inside as Magolino's soldiers ran to meet them, but they broke free with a monstrous *twang* that sounded like the largest mouth harp in creation.

"Head for the house!" Lanza ordered. "Faster!"

Grinning like a jackal now, his driver ground the truck's gearbox, speeding down the driveway toward the mansion. Lanza saw someone on the front porch staring at them, then the figure darted inside.

So much for his surprise. They'd kicked the hornet's nest, and soon the swarm would be upon them, stingers poised to strike. He snatched the walkie-talkie from his belt and started barking orders to his soldiers in the cargo vans.

"Be ready! We are almost at the portico! Now, jump! For *Cosa Nostra* and the honor of our family!"

Before the truck stopped moving, Lanza hit the pavement and sprinted toward the house.

"EASY," BOLAN SAID, when he felt his captive fidgeting. "Do you want to live?"

"Yes," the soldier said. "I'm taking you right to her."

"How much farther?"

"We're just coming to the stairs."

So, it would be the basement, as he'd guessed. "We get there," Bolan said, "and you go down first. One slip, you're history."

They reached the next-to-last door on their right, and Bolan's point man turned the knob. It opened inward on a flight of stairs descending steeply into semi-darkness. Dim light was showing at the lower level, but the soldier flipped a switch and turned on two caged bulbs above the staircase, letting them descend more confidently. Bolan

stayed two steps above his prisoner, in case the mobster
turned or tried to bolt, his finger steady on the Spectre's
trigger as they made their way downstairs.

"You know the lady, eh?" his captive asked.

"Shut up!" Bolan cautioned him.

"Okay. I only thought—"

A sharp rap with the Spectre's silencer cut off the soldier's running patter. At the bottom of the stairs they moved
along a spacious corridor chilled by the mansion's air con-
ditioning. It lacked the normal cellblock smell but had a
prison feel about it all the same. Bolan counted six doors
along the right-hand side.

"Which one?" he asked.

"The third one down, I think."

"Be sure. Your life depends on it."

"Okay, I'm sure."

When they reached the door in question, the soldier
stopped, muttered something and stood still with his shoulders slumped.

"What's that? Speak up!" Bolan commanded.

"I don't have the key, sir. Only *il padrino* can unlock
this one."

"I guess we're done then," Bolan said and put a silent
round behind his ear, dropping the mobster's carcass at his
feet. He dragged it clear, stepped up to the door and rapped
sharply on its surface with his knuckles. "Mariana?"

"Who is that?" the muffled voice came back.

"Scott Parker."

"Thank God! Hurry, please!"

"I have to blow the lock. Stand clear," he told her.

"I can't stand at all," she answered. "I'm tied up on the
bed."

"And where's that in relation to the door?"

"Directly opposite."

"Okay then. Close your eyes and turn your face away
if you can manage it."

"Hurry!" she said again. "He's coming back soon!"

Bolan blew the dead bolt from its mooring, tried the knob—still locked—and gave the door a solid kick that smashed it open and swung it back against the nearest wall. He spotted Mariana on the bed a second later, crossed to reach her there and opened his stiletto with a *snap* to cut her bonds. When she was free and on her feet, she threw her arms around him, trembling, sobbing out her gratitude.

"We'll talk about it later," Bolan said. "Right now, we have to move."

"Of course. But where—"

Excited voices in the hall outside cut short her question. Bolan went to check the doorway, saw two burly mobsters rushing toward him, then ducked backward as they opened fire with pistols. The gunfire echoed like thunder in the corridor.

14

Peppino Lanza's soldiers charged the mansion like a gang of madmen—howling and shooting—and it nearly worked. Lanza himself was on the porch and had nearly reached the tall front door before windows to either side of him erupted with a scalding blaze of gunfire, toppling half a dozen of his men in seconds flat.

The capo ducked and rolled, fetched up against the stucco wall with thunder ringing in his ears and watched as his surviving raiders scattered. Some ran back to crouch behind the trucks they had arrived in, seeking cover; others broke to left and right, trying to outrun bullets and escape the line of fire.

Lanza sat rock-still with his Beretta SMG pressed to his chest, afraid to move in case he drew attention to himself. The little stutter gun was empty, slide locked open on a smoking chamber, but reloading it meant pulling out the empty magazine, taking another from his pocket and inserting it, then drawing back the cocking handle. All of that meant noise, and at the moment, any sound could get him killed.

Instead, he slowly slipped a hand inside his rumpled jacket to retrieve the pistol holstered underneath his arm. It was a Beretta Px4 Storm, chambered in .40 S&W and loaded with ten hollow-point rounds. Not much in the face of a hostile army, but if Magolino's soldiers ventured onto the porch where Lanza sat, at least he could take a few of them with him.

This was what it came to, finally, and Lanza guessed no one would ever know that he'd done his best, had nearly penetrated Magolino's home before his soldiers either died or cut and ran. All that Alessandro Bevilacqua would remember of this escapade was that the leader of his Catanzaro crew had failed.

So be it. If he was condemned, Lanza decided, then he might as well make the most of it.

Setting his pistol down beside him, he withdrew the submachine gun's magazine and tossed it across the porch steps toward the driveway, where it clattered on asphalt. He drew another from one of his pockets, this one holding thirty rounds, and snapped it into the M12's receiver with a sharp metallic *click*.

Inside the house, behind the nearest shattered window, someone called attention to the sound. Another Magolino soldier answered. Lanza heard them shifting, moving toward the bullet-scarred front door.

"Come on, then," Lanza muttered. "Come and get me."

Noisily, defiantly, he cocked the submachine gun. Lanza clutched it in his right hand and retrieved the pistol with his left, then clambered to his feet and moved to stand before the mansion's entrance. Someone's bullets, possibly his own, had sprung the lock and left the door ajar an inch or two.

Smiling and mouthing prayers he hadn't uttered since he was eight or nine years old, Peppino Lanza kicked the door inward and followed through, guns blazing in both hands, trying his best to make each bullet count and feeling giddy from the chaos he was causing.

Some of Magolino's startled soldiers reeled and ran away from him, whereas others stood their ground. He shot them all impartially, watching the blood explode from stunned faces and lurching bodies, breathing in the heady reek of burnt gunpowder. When return fire started ripping into him, he barely felt it, living in a *Scarface* moment where the world was his and enemies must fall or bow before him.

He was laughing when the head shot came and all of it went black.

BOLAN UNCLIPPED A frag grenade, removed its pin, and held the striker lever down. Once he released it, he'd have about four seconds to get rid of the grenade, and that could vary by a full half second either way. No time to lose, in either case, as the two shooters kept advancing, spacing out their shots to keep Bolan from firing back.

He made the pitch, feeling a bullet pluck the cuff of his extended arm, then crouched and waited for the blast. It came on schedule, more or less, engulfing anguished screams from Magolino's dying men. When Bolan checked the corridor, he found it painted red, the smell of high explosives in his nostrils vying with the visceral aroma of dismantled human beings.

"Follow me," he ordered Mariana. "Never mind the smell or what you see."

"Good."

Despite her seeming confidence, there was a tremor in her voice, and Bolan heard her breath catch in her throat as she emerged into the charnel house.

"Remember that they kidnapped you and would have killed you," he advised her. "You're alive, and they're not. That's all."

"I understand," she answered, nearly choking on the words.

They reached the staircase, Bolan pausing to sling his Spectre, switching to the ARX-160. The time for stealth had passed. From now on, it was simple blast-your-ass-to-hell-and-back all the way.

But Mariana remained a problem.

He had rescued her a second time—or, rather, was at-

tempting to—but if he tried to get her off the property, that
meant truncating his assault on Magolino's family. Assuming it was even possible for both of them to make it out, an
early retreat left Bolan's work unfinished.

And he likely wouldn't get another chance.

"You know where the garage is?" he asked Mariana,
standing at the bottom of the stairs.

"I do."

"I want to stash you there for now. I still have work to
do."

"You'd leave me?" Panic in her voice.

"Listen—"

Before Bolan could finish, voices near the doorway
overhead forced him to take his own advice, ears straining to make out the words. Someone had heard the gun-
shots and grenade blast, obviously, but the comment Bolan
caught was curious.

"How did they get inside, downstairs?"

Before another voice replied, he heard the muffled
sounds of battle coming from a distance, probably outside
the Magolino mansion. His thoughts skipped to Peppino
Lanza and his *mafiosi* and Lanza's comment about going
after Magolino and the best man winning.

Unexpected help? He'd take whatever he could get.

"Stand back," he cautioned Mariana, then squeezed off
a 40 mm round that lofted through the upstairs doorway,
struck the wall directly opposite and detonated with a crack
of smoky thunder. "Now! Come on!"

He hammered up the stairs, with Mariana close on Bolan's heels, into another scene of carnage. Three men had
been standing in the hallway when his HE round went off,
and one of them was still alive, though barely hanging on,
riddled from knees to throat with shrapnel. His companions
both lay twisted where they'd fallen, weapons scattered on
the bloodstained carpet, and the sounds of gunfire from
outside were louder now.

"This way," Bolan said, turning to his right and leading Mariana toward an exit, which, he hoped, would place them reasonably close to the garage.

Or in the middle of a gangland firestorm.

Either way, he had to take the chance.

CAPTAIN BASILE BROKE every speed limit en route to Tropea, blue lights flashing the whole way from Catanzaro to the smaller town's outskirts, clearing slower traffic from his path. He met no State Police along the way and passed most of the other traffic as if it were standing still.

The trip was short at that speed, windows open, windrush nearly drowning out his thoughts. Basile had switched off the Bravo's two-way radio as soon as he decided on a course of action, severing his only link to headquarters. He might regret it later—part of him regretted it already—but he wouldn't let himself be interrupted now.

His Benelli shotgun lay across the empty seat beside him, braced on its boxes of spare cartridges to keep the gun from sliding.

Whatever else happened today, he would repay the pig Albanesi for the ambush that had nearly claimed his life, and in doing that, he'd wipe at least one small stain of corruption from the agency he'd served most of his adult life. If it cost Basile his career and pension—even if it cost his life—he thought he would be satisfied. As for the Magolino family, he was content to leave their fate in Scott Parker's hands.

Unless they tried to interfere with him.

The location of Magolino's country home was on file, and his GPS led him to the very gates of the estate. Basile was prepared to drive by casually, checking out the premises, but on arrival he discovered that the wrought-iron gate had been destroyed, apparently by impact from some large and heavy vehicle. Two bodies lay inside the yawning portal, asphalt darkened by their leaking blood.

Basile drove through, maneuvering around the bodies as he slowed for a closer look. Both men were obviously dead, their weapons left beside them on the pavement. Basile stopped on impulse, set the Bravo's parking brake and stepped out of the car to grab the two Kalashnikov assault rifles.

What could it hurt? More firepower increased his flagging confidence, and he didn't wish to find someone else aiming the rifles his way if he had to beat a swift retreat from Magolino's property.

He would have been trespassing, but the corpses gave him legal cause to investigate their slaying and search for other victims. Normally, he would have called for help from headquarters, both reinforcements and forensics experts to assess the evidence, but he was off the grid now, operating on his own initiative, unsanctioned. Nothing he did from that point on would qualify as by the book.

And damn it, that felt good.

As he was climbing back into the car, he heard echoes of gunfire from the general direction of the Magolino mansion straight ahead. Some kind of battle had been joined, and this would be the time to radio for units of the GDF's Rapid Response team if he wasn't going it alone. Even now, he could still call for help and explain the case later, but Basile was a stubborn man.

He would go in alone, with more guns than he could comfortably carry and hoping for the best.

Hoping, at least, to make it through the afternoon alive.

FRESH AIR AND sunshine greeted Bolan as he slipped out through a rear exit from Magolino's sprawling home with Mariana on his heels and maintaining contact with a hand at Bolan's waist. He scanned the sweeping lawn in front of him for enemies, found none immediately visible and started off toward the garage.

The long, low building stood twenty-odd yards from

the house, all but one of its doors lowered. The open door revealed a royal blue Jaguar XKR 75, the limited edition, standing ready to eat up the highway if Bolan could get it started. And behind the other doors? So far, a mystery.

When they'd covered half the distance, Bolan glanced back toward the front gate and saw it had been battered down. A small sedan had just pulled through and was proceeding toward the house, the face of its lone occupant concealed behind the tinted windshield. Even so, he saw the rack of lights on top and recognized the Fiat Bravo as a standard-issue GDF vehicle.

One cop, passing by the scene and drawn in by the evidence of violence? Maybe an officer summoned by Magolino, hoping he could help somehow? Or could it be…

Bolan had not tipped off Captain Basile when he left Catanzaro, hoping he could finish up his business and be gone before any police arrived. Now, with one cop on the scene and others likely following, he had no time to waste.

Bolan slipped into the garage, with Mariana following. He checked the car and found a key in its ignition. "Can you drive this?" he inquired.

Even beat-up and terrified, she managed a disdainful look. "Of course."

"All right. The gate's clear. Get away from here as fast and far as possible and without involving the police."

"And you?" she asked, already opening the driver's door.

"I'm not done here," he told her. "And I've got a ride."

She hesitated, pecked him on the cheek then slid behind the Jaguar's steering wheel and fired the engine with a throaty snarl of power. Seconds later, she was smoking toward the twisted wrought-iron gate without a backward glance.

He wished the lady luck, reckoned she'd need it however the current fight went down, then turned back to the task at hand. He could no longer see the lone police car. But Bolan refused to let himself be sidetracked looking for the cop and turned back toward the house with his primary mission fixed in mind.

Find Magolino and his underboss, Adamo. Take them out, together with as many 'Ndrangheta soldiers as he could. Beyond that, getting out alive would be a bonus.

He was halfway back from the garage, retracing the path he'd followed with Mariana, when a group of four 'ndranghetisti came around the mansion's southwest corner, pissed off and looking for someone to kill.

Bolan shouldered his rifle and went back to war.

WHEN THE SHOOTING STARTED, Carlo Albanesi knew he had a choice to make. One option—staying in the library, waiting for someone to come by and kill him—was not viable. Leaving, however, meant going out alone, into a battle zone, unrecognized by those engaged on either side.

Except for Aldo and his boss, of course, who might want Albanesi dead.

The ex-lieutenant wished he was thinner, with less of him to hide as he was sneaking from the mansion out onto the grounds. Where would he go from there? His car had probably been moved away from Magolino's portico, stashed God knew where. If he was forced to flee on foot, his chances of survival would be reduced dramatically—but what else could he do?

Drawing his pistol, Albanesi crossed to the library door, opened it cautiously, listened, then peered outside. The sounds of battle, louder now, made Albanesi fret that he might soil himself. His only past exposure to gunfire was on the practice range, and when a loud explosion rocked the house, his heart leaped to his throat. His feet seemed rooted to the carpet, but he knew he was running out of time.

Go now! a voice inside his head commanded, and he bolted from the library.

Which way? He'd come in through the front door, where the battle sounds were loudest. Accordingly, he turned left as he exited, putting the parlor and the portico behind him, rushing down the hall toward—what?

A lowly pawn in Magolino's empire, Albanesi had not been invited to the godfather's estate, had never been inside the house or roamed the wooded grounds. Logic advised him there had to be more exits to a house this large, and he would find one if he kept on searching, dodging enemies along the way and shooting anyone who threatened him.

But could he bring himself to pull the trigger on a living target?

Yes, he thought, if it was all that stood between himself and death. He'd trained for situations such as this, like every other law enforcement officer, although he'd never actually thought one would occur.

Halfway along the corridor, he passed a kitchen and was drawn to the fragrant smells of roasting meat and pasta on the stove. He cursed his stomach as it grumbled a request for sustenance. No time, for God's sake!

He did not check the other doors along the corridor, assuming they opened onto rooms without a way to the outside. So far, he'd met no challenges, no soldiers. If his luck held, it would stay that way, and once he got outside, he could retreat into the woods he'd noticed on arrival, maybe hide there until more police arrived, then flash his badge and try to pass himself off as a member of the team. Maybe pick up one of their cars and slip away while they were busy sorting out the chaos.

Beyond that, his mind went blank.

With Magolino and Adamo gone—or, at the very least, detained for questioning—he had no one to ask for help. He had a bank account under another name in Reggio Calabria, if he could get to it. From there, maybe a boat to Sicily, some forged I.D. and a search for somewhere in the world to hide.

But he would have to take it one step at a time and do whatever was required to stay alive.

BOLAN SLAMMED A double-tap into the nearest gunman's chest, then tracked from left to right across the ragged skirmish line. The second soldier got a shot off as he fell, spilling his blood onto the lawn, his bullet wasted on a clear blue sky. The others broke and ran for cover and quickly discovered there was none.

Bolan shot the farthest runner first, a 5.56 mm round between his shoulder blades that picked him up, then slammed him facedown to the ground, twitching the final seconds of his life away. The last one nearly made it to the house, was scrabbling at a locked window when Bolan dropped him with a head shot from a range of fifty feet. His bright blood stained the glass and blotched the beige stucco as he went down.

Double-timing toward the mansion, Bolan let fly with a 40 mm round, punching it through the bloodstained window where the dead 'ndranghetisti has spent his last seconds scratching at impassive glass. The high-explosive round detonated inside, spewing smoke and dust from the window frame onto the lawn. He dodged the flying shrapnel, got to the exit where he'd left the house with Mariana and ducked back inside.

Chaos and cursing, cries of anguish, gunfire echoing through spacious rooms, smoke in the air. It added up to a familiar scene—Old Home Week for the Executioner.

He sought Gianni Magolino now, ranking his underboss as second prize. Beyond those two, the rest were simply pop-up targets in a shooting gallery. If he encountered Lanza's men along the way, fighting against the 'Ndrangheta, he would show them no more mercy than he felt for the initial targets of his probe.

It was a fire sale. Everything—and everyone—must go.

Right now, he needed someone who would talk to him, direct him to the men in charge. An aimless search through countless rooms was worse than futile. It would waste his precious time, while giving Magolino and Adamo opportunity to flee.

Unacceptable.

The trick would be to take one of the home team by surprise, subdue him without any lethal damage and convince him that survival hinged on spilling anything Bolan could use within the next few minutes to complete his mission. And if that proved to be a lie, what of it in the midst of all-out war?

What else could any adversary hope for in a battle to the death?

He pushed on through the smoky haze, hunting.

And swiftly running out of time.

15

Captain Basile drove into a slaughterhouse. Two moving vans were parked in front of Magolino's mansion with their engines running, paint and windscreens scarred by bullets, bodies huddled on the nearby pavement. Who were these intruders, shot down in their tracks before they reached the house?

Why should he even care?

To some extent, he viewed the underworld as a self-cleaning oven. Sadly, its flames consumed innocents in the process, and the cleansing was never completed because new scum rose up to replace the old.

Perhaps today, that balance might be shifted.

He took the shotgun with him, flicking off its safety with his thumb as he stepped out of the Fiat Bravo. The cargo vans concealed him briefly from the view of any gunmen covering the mansion's front windows, but Basile could not linger there. If he were to have any hope of finding Carlo Albanesi, he'd need to do it on the move, risking his life with every step.

But was the porcine traitor worth it?

Too late, now, for him to reconsider. If he'd turned back at Magolino's gate, perhaps, but now…

Basile moved around the van parked to his left, edging along its side and drawing closer to the house. It seemed to him that gunfire came from somewhere in the house itself, a battle going on inside, even though it looked as if a first attempt to penetrate the dwelling had been foiled.

He had nearly reached the cab when a frantic-looking gunman stumbled out in front of him and stopped dead, eyeing Basile and his shotgun with a shocked expression. The younger man was armed, a semiautomatic pistol in his left hand, but he seemed to have forgotten it at the sight of Basile.

The spell broke when Basile shifted slightly, leveling his shotgun at the other man's midsection. With a raspy shout, the gunman tried to raise his weapon, but Basile got there first, a blast of buckshot from his twelve-gauge opening the wiry mobster's stomach, spraying blood and mangled viscera; its odor mixed with gunsmoke to assault Basile's nostrils.

His fifth killing within a single day did not disturb Basile. Rather, he felt numb, beyond shock or the other symptoms commonly attributed to persons who had taken human life. He drew no pleasure from the killing; it simply felt like…nothing.

Seven rounds were left in the shotgun as Basile edged around the truck's cab and craned his neck to see the mansion's entrance. No one shot his head off, and he took that as a bonus. He had an awkward moment, almost stumbling on the corpse he'd made, but kept his balance with an effort and moved on. He reached the broad front steps, took them two at a time, and found himself before the open door, its lock blown free by point-blank gunfire.

Basile hesitated for a heartbeat then went inside. More leaking corpses stained the floor in front of him, fouling the air. The worst of them—shot several dozen times, with half its face missing—still sparked something within the captain's memory. He'd seen that partial face before, undoubtedly.

Peppino Lanza? It was possible, although Basile could not swear to it.

But if it *was* Lanza, what was the mafioso doing here, inside Gianni Magolino's country home?

The simple answer seemed to be having his brains blown out, but what had brought him to that point? Basile realized it made no difference any longer, and he moved on past the bodies, some of them presumably gunned down by Lanza while he lived.

The battle beckoned, and Basile suddenly discovered he couldn't wait.

BOLAN FOUND HIS pigeon hiding in a closet, whimpering. The twenty-something mobster seemed to be having a breakdown. Huddled in a corner of the closet with a Heckler & Koch MP5 submachine gun sitting in his lap, he made no attempt to raise it when he saw Bolan's ARX-160 leveled at his tear-streaked face.

"Please! Don't shoot me!"

"I need information," Bolan said.

"What information?" The kid seemed eager to please.

"Your bosses. Magolino and Adamo. Where are they?"

It was a long shot, Bolan realized, expecting help from a deserter, but if this one couldn't help him, he'd keep looking for a goon who could.

"They're leaving," the young man said.

"When? Where are they going?"

"They don't tell me nothing," he half sobbed. "I plead to go along with them, but Aldo slaps me. Says, 'Defend the family.' I should have shot that bastard."

He started to raise the SMP until Bolan said, "Watch it!"

"I'm sorry!" One of the quaking hands pushed the weapon off his lap and across the closet floor toward Bolan.

"How are they leaving?" Bolan asked.

"Taking a car, I think. They run away and leave me here to die."

A car. That meant they'd be heading back to the garage unless they had another motor pool he hadn't seen.

"From the garage?" he prodded.

"I think so." The kid was down to guessing now.

"Okay, then," Bolan said. Without another word he rapped the butt of his weapon against the young man's skull, knocking him to the floor, unconscious.

Bolan had seen no trace of Magolino or Adamo when he'd taken Mariana out to the garage, and he was reasonably sure they hadn't fled the property before she took off in the Jaguar. If he'd missed them somehow in his travels back and forth between the mansion and garage, they could be getting in a car that very moment, maybe halfway to the open gate by now.

Cursing, he turned and sprinted back the way he'd come, frustration mixing with adrenaline to boost his throbbing pulse. If Magolino got away…

Not this time.

Passing the open kitchen door, Bolan fired a 40 mm thermobaric round toward the industrial-size stove then continued on his way. The flames would spread in nothing flat and hopefully consume the house before they finally burned out. If his informant had been off the mark and Magolino still remained somewhere inside the mansion, maybe he'd go up in smoke.

But Bolan wanted to be sure. He *needed* to be sure.

A roiling cloud of smoke trailed Bolan as he exited the big house for the second time. He faced the garage and saw a second of its large doors standing open, displaying a black SUV in the bay. As he moved in that direction, one of the SUV's doors opened, turning on the interior dome light. Bolan caught a glimpse of Magolino's craggy face in profile as he slid into the shotgun seat, then slammed his door and killed the light.

Bolan sprinted off to intercept his quarry.

"THAT GODDAMNED LANZA!" Magolino snarled. "I should have known this was all his fault."

"All?" Adamo echoed. "Even the American?"

"To hell with the American! He's just someone Lanza hired to keep us guessing and confused."

Adamo was not convinced, but he was wise enough to avoid contradicting his *padrino,* particularly when Don Magolino was in such an agitated state. The wrong word now—even a sideways look—might set him off, and because the boss was carrying an Uzi SMG, making him angry could prove to be Adamo's last mistake.

They'd made it from the house to the garage all right, delayed in their departure because Magolino had insisted on going to finish the woman himself. Instead, they'd found her cell empty, with the remains of family soldiers spattered around the hallway outside, walls scorched and pocked with shrapnel from the blast that killed them. Some kind of grenade, Adamo thought, remembering the blast that had rocked the mansion moments before he and Magolino began their trek downstairs.

Finding the woman had escaped a second time, the boss had nearly lost it. When he'd regained enough composure to speak rationally, Magolino had demanded they search the house and grounds for Mariana, track her down and kill her as a matter of honor, but Adamo had dissuaded him, eventually convincing Magolino that discretion was the better part of valor.

They must live to fight another day and settle their accounts when it was safe.

Or, at the very least, saf*er.*

Then they had fled, taking one bodyguard with them, all three armed with automatic weapons. They'd slipped out of the mansion, briefly delayed by a quaking young soldier who'd begged to accompany them, then made for the seven-car garage at top speed, with the guard covering their retreat.

Adamo thought he should feel guilty about running out on their surviving soldiers, but he found it didn't bother him at all. His job was looking out for Number One—in this case, Magolino—with himself ranked Number Two.

And what if he was forced to choose between his own life and the godfather's?

In that case, he supposed, *il padrino* was shit out of luck.

Magolino was shocked to find his Jaguar XKR missing. The discovery touched off another raging fit of profanity and pointless questions. Who had taken the car? Where had they gone? Adamo didn't know and could not have cared less, as long as he got off the premises alive.

He opened the next garage door in line, revealing the sleek black form of a Lexus RX 450h sport utility vehicle. Magolino kept all of his vehicles polished, fueled and with their keys in the ignition, acting on the theory that no one would dare steal from him. The missing Jaguar disproved that hypothesis, but the Lexus comfortably seated four, and it would get them back to Catanzaro—or some other destination Magolino might demand—in air-conditioned style.

"Come on!" Magolino urged them. "Hurry up!"

Adamo was already hurrying, but it would do no good to say so. As he climbed into the backseat, with their bodyguard behind the wheel and Magolino at his side, the 'Ndrangheta underboss allowed himself to breathe a little easier. They had a chance now—to escape, to live, to fight another day.

He thought of Albanesi then, forgotten in the library, and glanced back toward the house, where flames were leaping from the windows. Was the fat lieutenant trapped inside? Was he still waiting for his audience with Magolino?

Aldo shrugged it off. Roast pork was not his problem at the moment.

"Go! Go!" Magolino urged their driver, slapping his shoulder for emphasis. The Lexus rolled forward, gathering speed—then stopped dead.

In front of them, a solitary gunman stood his ground,

eyeing the SUV. If Aldo had to guess, he would have said the stranger looked American.

"What are you waiting for?" Magolino snapped. "Run him down!"

BOLAN HEARD THE SUV's engine revving into red-line levels, and he saw three pairs of eyes glaring at him through the broad tinted windshield. The SUV lurched forward suddenly, tires squealing on the concrete floor of the garage as it launched toward Bolan and gathering momentum by the heartbeat. If he dodged now, Magolino could be past him by the time he managed target acquisition, maybe ruining the shot.

Bolan stood fast and squeezed the 40 mm launcher's trigger, sending a high-explosive round to meet the charging SUV. It struck the black car's grille, an inch or so below the stylized "L" that told him he was firing on a Lexus, fifty grand and change with all the bells and whistles and hurtling toward him with a mind to plow him under like a weed.

The blast was nearly deafening at such close range. The SUV stood on its nose, engulfed in smoke and flames, its rear end rising as if the driver had crashed headlong into a concrete wall. From there, momentum flipped it over, crashing down toward Bolan as he finally ducked to his left and let the tumbling four-door pass him by, trailing its comet's tail of fire.

Touchdown popped the SUV open and sent three ragdoll figures tumbling over pavement, weapons clattering away from hands that couldn't keep their grip. Bolan saw the driver fetch up on his left side, head canted at an impossible angle that told him the guy's neck was broken. Off to the SUV's left side—his right—Gianni Magolino and Aldo Adamo were both still alive, though Adamo's left leg now displayed an extra bend that would have startled Mother Nature.

Bolan moved to catch the 'Ndrangheta's underboss in midscream, as the man reached for his broken leg, and silenced him forever with a NATO round between the eyes. That left Magolino, clearly the toughest of the SUV's passengers, struggling to all fours as he watched the Executioner approach.

The mobster spat blood and demanded, "How much is that rat Peppino paying you for this?"

"I never met the man," Bolan replied. "But if I see him, he'll be right behind you. That's a promise."

"So, he didn't hire you?" Magolino looked confused.

"Not even close," Bolan said. "This is for the marshals your men murdered in New York."

"Marshals? Those peasants? Are you crazy?"

"It's been said, by other dead men like yourself."

"All this for those two-bit cops?" The mobster shook his head in wonderment, blood dripping from his chin. "I take that as an insult!"

"Take it any way you like," Bolan said and stitched a 3-round burst across his final target's chest. The slugs punched Magolino over backward, landing with his legs folded beneath him, which would have hurt him terribly if he were still alive.

"Good shooting," said a voice behind him. "Now be smart, and drop the rifle."

CARLO ALBANESI COULD not believe his good fortune. He hadn't expected to escape from Magolino's home alive, trapped as he'd been between hostile hosts and attackers who seemed bent on killing everyone inside the mansion. But the initial phase of his escape had proved relatively simple. It appeared that he'd been forgotten in the library when the attack began, and that worked to his favor. Slipping out of there, unseen, he'd suffered several moments of confusion, then nearly collided with a young man carrying a submachine gun, who stopped short and covered Albanesi with the weapon, asking him, "Who the hell are you?"

"A friend of Aldo's," Albanesi said. "I mean, Mr. Adamo."

The soldier blinked at him then said, "If you're trying to catch him, you're late. He's already left with *il padrino.*"

"Left?" A surge of panic had enveloped Albanesi. "Where did they go?"

"The garage, I suppose. Getting out."

The gunman was turning away when Albanesi took a chance and caught him by the sleeve. "Which way, please?" he asked.

The soldier made an irritated clucking sound and pointed vaguely to his right, the same direction Albanesi had been headed when they met. Then he was gone, no further opportunity to question him or get precise directions. Albanesi had been somewhat amazed to find an exit from the mansion sixty seconds later.

Facing the garage, he'd been in time to see Adamo, Magolino and a bodyguard slip inside. From somewhere to his left, another figure tracked them, this one dressed in military-style fatigues and laden with weapons. For a moment, Albanesi thought some kind of SWAT team had arrived—the Carabinieri Special Operations Group, perhaps, or the GDF's own Antiterrorism and Rapid Response service—but this man, clearly, was alone.

And then it hit him: the American!

Albanesi watched as the tall man stalked his prey, moving to intercept Magolino and Adamo in their getaway car. The wise thing, he supposed, would be to run the other way and let them slaughter one another, hopefully forgetting all about Albanesi in the process. But the scene fascinated him, and he could not tear his eyes away.

He saw the Lexus SUV charge forward, saw the bold American stop it with some kind of rocket or grenade then walk around and finish off the men who had been thrown clear of the flaming wreckage. By that time, against his conscious will, the ex-lieutenant's feet were taking him directly toward the killing ground, approaching from the grim-faced killer's blind side.

Dredging up his voice while covering the stranger with his sidearm, Albanesi said, "Good shooting. "Now be smart, and drop the rifle."

BOLAN TURNED SLOWLY, rifle still in hand, and saw a fat man in a rumpled suit pointing a pistol at his face. The guy was nervous, gun hand trembling, and his eyes flicked spastically, trying to cover every angle of the scene at once.

"Who are you?" Bolan asked.

Fumbling underneath his jacket with his free hand, the new arrival flashed a wallet, showing off a badge and I.D. card. "Lieutenant Albanesi of the Guardia di Finanza," he replied. "And you, I think, are Scott Parker."

"Never met the man," Bolan said.

"We shall see. First thing, you need to drop your weapon. Make that *weapons*. All of them."

"And if I don't?"

"Then I will kill you. Either way, I am the hero of the hour. It's ironic, eh?"

Bolan had no idea what that meant, so he let it go. This was the worst scenario of any mission, running up against his own rule about police. Without that self-imposed restriction, Bolan knew he could have taken this one, even covered as he was. A feint, a duck, a quick shot from the hip, and he'd be clear.

Not happening.

But going into custody meant death at some point, likely sooner rather than later. He'd be disavowed by Stony Man and every other U.S. agency, covert or public. The publicity could damage Hal, the program Bolan served, his very reason for existing.

"So, you want to be a hero?" Bolan inquired.

"It's an attractive option," the fat man said. "If you only knew my problems, but they're none of your concern. The rifle first. Be careful when you set it down."

Surrender? Or a suicide by cop? He wondered if the lieutenant's hand was firm enough to kill him with a single shot, or if he'd need a whole damned magazine to finish it.

"Well?" Albanesi challenged him.

"I'm thinking," Bolan said. And he was watching, too, tracking another figure coming toward them, double-timing over fresh-mown grass. "Is this a friend of yours?" he asked.

"Oh, no. I can't be tricked that easily," the cop replied. "I'm not—"

"Lieutenant!" the new arrival said, slowing as he reached them, balancing a semiauto shotgun in his hands.

"Captain Basile? What are you— I mean, it's fortunate that you've arrived."

"Indeed," the captain said. "Now, I will take charge of your weapon and your prisoner."

"Will you?" Albanesi bristled, small eyes darting back and forth between his adversaries. "And if I refuse?"

The shotgun blast, from ten feet out, lifted the fat man off his feet and dropped him on his back, gasping his final breath on impact. Bolan stood watching as Basile turned to face him with a frown, and the muzzle of his shotgun sagged.

"He was a useless bastard anyway," Basile said.

"Wanted to be a hero," Bolan told him.

"And perhaps he shall be after the reports are sanitized. It would not be the strangest thing that's ever happened, eh?"

"What now?"

"Is she here?" Basile asked. "Our Mariana?"

"You just missed her," Bolan said. "Before you ask, she didn't tell me where she was going."

"Just as well. It seems I can't be trusted to protect her."

"I suppose you did your best."

"Not good enough." Basile paused, glanced back toward Magolino's burning house, then said, "Don't you have somewhere else to be?"

"Now that you mention it."

"I have a good friend at headquarters," Basile said. "In records. I can almost guarantee your dossier will disappear."

"Almost?"

"Consider it a parting gift. As for the 'Ndrangheta—" he surveyed the scattered bodies "—I suspect they have forgotten you already."

"If you're sure…"

"Go with God, my friend."

Bolan turned and left Basile there, retreating toward the tree line as a pall of smoke descended over Magolino's grand estate. He might not go with God—who really had a claim on that?—but he had caught a lucky break, and he'd live to fight another day.

Likely tomorrow or the next day, when the names and faces changed, but Bolan knew the stakes would always be the same. Good versus evil, life or death. He raised on every hand, the only way he knew to play the game.

All in.

Epilogue

Leonardo da Vinci–Fiumicino Airport, Rome

Bolan played it safe, using his backup passport to avoid relying on the Parker name while Captain Basile was purging the GDF's files. He'd flown out of Reggio Calabria's Tito Minniti Airport and landed in Rome without incident. Even then, he was watchful, aware that Basile might fail—or simply change his mind—and the net could drop at any moment.

He'd been in touch with Hal, briefly, by scrambled sat phone to explain the situation as it stood. Brognola grumbled, as expected, but agreed that they should wait and see what happened in the next few days before they wiped Bolan's alias off the books. The GDF captain had proved himself by saving Bolan's bacon in a pinch, and if his follow-through was verified by Stony Man's elite crew of hackers, "Scott Parker" could return to action in due time.

Meanwhile, Bolan ate pasta and eggplant parmesan at the airport, cooled his heels and waited for his transatlantic Alitalia flight to JFK. He bought a fat paperback to fill any time he didn't spend sleeping in transit and got through one chapter before thoughts of his mission distracted him.

Bolan would probably never know what became of Mariana Natale, whether Magolino's successors ignored her or spent their time hunting her down. The lady could make her own choices, for good or ill, and her fate was out of Bolan's hands.

Captain Basile was a little easier. With help from Hal and Stony Man, Bolan could keep track of the officer if he was so inclined. But to what end? Their worlds had intersected for a fleeting moment, but they likely never would again.

The news on television, broadcast through the airport concourse, played up the Tropea massacre and stressed the death of a "heroic" GDF officer, as Basile had predicted. Higher-ups were covering themselves, whitewashing the force and its bad apple to defer any further scrutiny. Bolan had seen the same thing happen elsewhere many times before, from New York City and L.A. to London and Paris.

Spin was in and always would be. After all, self-preservation was the first rule of politics. Some things never changed, and Bolan understood that all too well.

It was the reason the world needed the Executioner.

* * * * *

The Executioner®
Don Pendleton's

SAVAGE DEADLOCK

No Man's Land

A missing US nuclear scientist resurfaces as a member of a guerrilla women's rights organization in Pakistan, raising all kinds of alarms in Washington and gaining the attention of rebel fighters.

GOLD EAGLE®

Mack Bolan is tasked with extracting the woman and getting her Stateside, even if she doesn't want to go. But as the rebels close in and the guerrilla group realizes it's weaker than the trained fighters, Bolan and a handful of allies are forced to join the battle. Their team might be small, but the Executioner has might on his side.

Available January 2015
wherever books and ebooks are sold.

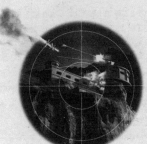